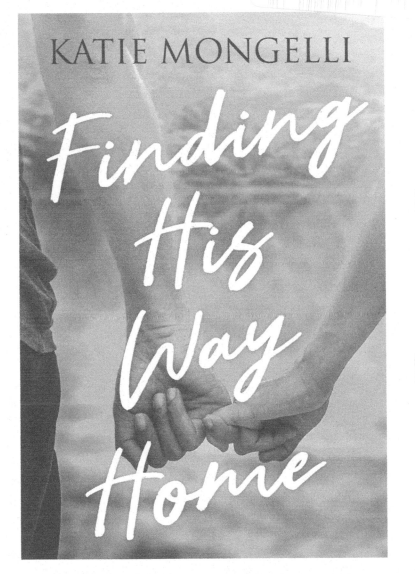

KATIE MONGELLI

Finding His Way Home

Finding His Way Home

KATIE MONGELLI

woodhall press

Woodhall Press | Norwalk, CT

Woodhall Press, 81 Old Saugatuck Road, Norwalk, CT 06855
WoodhallPress.com

Cover design: Asha Hossain
Layout artist: L.J. Mucci

Library of Congress Cataloging-in-Publication Data available

ISBN 978-1-954907-84-3   (paper: alk paper)
ISBN 978-1-954907-85-0   (electronic)

First Edition
Distributed by Independent Publishers Group
(800) 888-4741

Printed in the United States of America

For MeMa who taught me to love the adventure of life.

Chapter 1

Zach Hartmann sits at a table facing the judge's imposing bench and watches the court reporter furiously tapping the keys of her stenograph, trying to keep up with everything being said. Discreetly, he rubs his sweaty hand along his thigh, hoping to stop his leg from shaking.

"All rise for the Honorable Judge Charles White," the deputy clerk announces, bringing the whole room to their feet. "*United States v. Zachary Hartmann.*"

"Mr. Hartmann, have you been furnished with a copy of the motion to freeze your assets, which has been filed by the plaintiff?" Judge White asks.

Clearing his throat and hoping his voice wouldn't fail him, he answers, "Yes, Your Honor."

"I'm not going to read the entire document, but Mr. Hartmann, I want to make sure you understand that a motion has been filed to freeze all of your financial assets pending trial, in which you are being charged with making false statements, as well as mail and wire fraud. Both are felony offenses. Do you understand, sir?"

"Yes, Your Honor, I do."

At six-foot-four, Zach towers over everyone in the courtroom. He buttons his suit coat and squares his broad shoulders, ready for the judge's ruling. Sneaking a glance at his lawyer, Scott Campbell, he sees a man who looks calm and collected, with his hands clasped behind his back, and follows suit.

The federal prosecutor to his right adjusts his striped tie and writes notes on his yellow legal pad. Zach wants to hate this man who is out to ruin his life, but he looks just like any other man in his forties. He could be someone's husband or father.

The federal prosecutor stands and begins his argument. "Your Honor, the shareholders suffered financial losses in excess of one hundred million dollars. Now these innocent victims are left wondering how they are going to pay for their children's college tuition, or how they'll be able to retire. Our evidence proves that Mr. Hartmann knew the audited financial statements in this prospectus were inaccurate, but he continued to promote the merger and mislead investors, directly causing them financial harm."

Scott stands. "Your Honor, there is no evidence that my client intended to deceive the shareholders, or that Mr. Hartmann's activities caused their financial losses."

"Your Honor, that isn't accurate. We have witnesses that will prove Mr. Hartmann was not just involved, but that he orchestrated this fraud."

Scott looks at Zach and mutters under his breath, "What is he talking about?"

"I didn't orchestrate anything," Zach snaps back in a whisper.

"Your Honor, I have reviewed the prosecution's witness list and I have serious doubts about the integrity of their testimony," says Scott. "I think we all know the guilty party isn't even here today. The United States is using my client, Mr. Hartmann, as a scapegoat. I think it is time the United States does their job and brings Mr. Anderson in."

"Mr. Hartmann has substantial financial means, and we believe he will leave the country and evade prosecution if his assets aren't frozen," the prosecutor argues.

"Mr. Hartmann is a man of integrity and has every intention of showing up to clear his name," Scott barks at the prosecutor.

"The defendant will remain free on bail. The plaintiff's motion to freeze assets is granted. Court is adjourned," the judge announces, pounding his gavel.

While everyone else is prompted into motion, immediately scurrying forward with other business, Zach stands frozen, gasping, as if all the air has been knocked out of him.

That's it? Zach thinks, falling back into his chair. Scott had outlined how the hearing would go, but he thought there would be a longer discussion of the matter. He had been confident that once the judge heard their compelling arguments, he would rule in their favor.

Zach sits motionless. He feels a hand squeezing his shoulder. It's Scott, pulling him back into reality.

"Come on, let's go," he says, snapping his briefcase shut.

Zach follows Scott out of the courtroom. He sees Scott's lips moving but doesn't hear the words.

"What just happened?" Zach asks.

"This was just a pretrial conference. You know this is going to be a long road," Scott says.

"What am I going to do?" Zach says, more to himself than Scott.

"We'll figure that out later. Look, the press is circling like sharks, so keep your head down, your mouth shut, and stick close to me."

3

They step outside the courthouse doors shoulder to shoulder and are immediately bombarded by the clicking of cameras and reporters calling out "Zach! Zach! How do you feel about the judge's decision?"

Zach pauses momentarily to watch the federal prosecutor approach the podium, set up for the media conference in front of the courthouse.

"This is the biggest corporate fraud the people of Minnesota have suffered in decades, and we are pleased with the judge's decision today. We are going to pursue the most severe penalties—up to thirty years in prison and a five-million-dollar fine. We trust justice will be served swiftly . . ."

Zach blocks out the rest.

Across the street angry protesters chant and wave signs that read "Crime doesn't pay!" and "Give us our money back!" A mounted police officer walks his horse back and forth in front of the crowd, keeping them behind the blockade so they don't charge the courthouse.

Zach's heart drops as he looks at the faces of ordinary citizens who lost money because of this deal. *I didn't steal your money*, he wishes he could shout to them, but instead he turns away and continues to the car.

"Zach, will you be making a statement?" one reporter asks, shoving a microphone in his face.

He feels Scott's arm around his shoulders, pulling him toward the car, so he looks down at his feet, following Scott's guidance.

"No comment," Scott replies as he pushes his way through the sea of reporters and opens the door of the black sedan, waiting for Zach to climb in.

As they pull away, Zach can't help but watch the faces of the angry mob.

"I didn't do anything wrong," he says, looking over to Scott.

"Uh-huh," Scott says, sounding like he doesn't quite believe him. "Listen, they're angry and hurting. I get it—you're a good guy—but

I'm going to need something more. Our justice system requires hard evidence."

"What happened to innocent until proven guilty? My life is over. How can they do this to me?"

Looking at the protesters, Zach sighs, wishing they understood that he is just an innocent victim whose life is being destroyed, just like theirs. He has no career; and now, with his assets frozen, he has no money. His life is over before it really had a chance to begin.

He rests his head against the window and closes his eyes. The vibration of the car lulls him into a meditative state.

"I know today's decision was a blow," Scott says.

Zach slides farther down in his seat and crosses his arms over his chest.

"I need to know exactly what happened," Scott says. "No BS."

"How can Mr. Anderson go into hiding and leave me with all of this to clean up?" Zach asks.

"I can't believe you are a grown man calling your boss 'mister,' like he's some fourth-grade math teacher," Scott teases. "Did he send you to detention?"

Zach opens his eyes long enough to glare at Scott.

"Come on, man. I'm just trying to lighten the mood here," says Scott. "I've known you since college, and I've watched you try to stick your head in the sand when there is trouble. I don't care what Bill did. All I care about is what you knew, and when you knew it. You've gotta give me something to work with."

"I don't know." Zach sighs. He sits up and looks out the window at the buildings downtown. He tries to think back to when they started this deal, two years ago.

"I thought a sixty percent increase in sales was unusual, but whenever I asked too many questions, he told me to mind my own business," Zach explains.

"Listen, everything is going to come out in the courtroom. What are you holding back? You'd better tell me now."

"The financials were audited by the CPAs. They're the experts on the numbers, not me. I'm just an MBA. Maybe Mr. Anderson was right, and I don't know how financials work," Zach answers, throwing up his arms.

Scott raises his eyebrows, not bothering to respond.

The car pulls over to the curb of the departures area of the Minneapolis–St. Paul International Airport.

"What are we doing here? We need to get to the office and strategize how to free up my assets."

Scott says, "Look, I think maybe some time away will help."

"No! We need a plan to put an end to this trial!" Zach shouts.

"Go home to Pine Lake and clear your head. I need you to be prepared. Trust me."

"Pine Lake?" Zach groans.

"Your assets are frozen," Scott says. "Where else did you have in mind?"

Zach rakes his fingers through his sandy blond hair. His broad shoulders slump, considering this new reality.

"Go see your dad," Scott says.

"Given the choice, I'd rather face the press."

"You sure about that?" Scott opens his briefcase and hands him an envelope. "I have taken care of everything. Go talk to him."

Zach opens the envelope holding his flight and rental car reservations and some cash.

"What? I can't I don't have anything with me."

"Do you have a better idea?"

Zach's cheeks redden and he shoves the envelope into his suit pocket. Turning to his friend, he pulls him in for a hug before starting toward the terminal.

"And stay away from Tracey," Scott calls after him.

Zach spins on a heel. "Why are you so hard on her?"

Scott looks around and says, "Do you see her here with you today? I don't. She is only worried about herself, and right now I'm worried about you."

Zach waves him off and heads into the terminal.

He gets through security relatively quickly, and soon, he's boarding the plane and crawls into his cramped window seat. From the ground the sky had looked gray and gloomy, but as the plane ascends, the thick pillow of clouds offers a heavenly view where legal and financial problems don't exist. As the plane heads east, the sky changes from blue to deep pinks and oranges as the sun sets.

How many nights had he watched evening fall over Lake Harriet from Mr. Anderson's yacht? He had been Mr. Anderson's golf caddy at the club for more than six years the first time he was invited on a sail. It was the summer before his senior year at the University of Minnesota.

When he first met Mr. Anderson, he'd never been sailing, or even imagined the kind of lifestyle Mr. Anderson lived. It wasn't what he'd expected. Stepping on board, he was greeted with a glass of champagne. At the back of the boat, which he later learned was the stern, party music blared as Mr. Anderson's daughter and her friends danced in their bikinis. Inside the cabin Mr. Anderson and his associates were playing poker and smoking cigars. Their slender and perfectly manicured wives were all sunning themselves on the front deck.

Zach awkwardly joined the card game, unsure how to behave. He grew up with a mother that clipped coupons and brought home hand-me-down clothes from church. Summers were spent collecting vegetables from the garden so his grandma could can them for the winter. All he'd known was that you earn an honest day's pay for an honest day's work. They didn't spend their Sundays drinking champagne and sailing on the lake.

When Mr. Anderson introduced him to his business partners Zach realized that this life could be an option for him. He was seduced by their level of confidence and material comforts, and accepted their job offer immediately. He was soon a regular at the poker game, talking deals.

If I could go back and jump off that boat, I wouldn't be in this mess today. He drops his head in his hands and rubs his temples. While he had been seduced by all the material comforts, he really wanted the whole package. He had pictured the career, the wealth, the loving and beautiful wife, a bubbly toddler bouncing on his shoulders on their way to a Saturday picnic by the water.

Now, the prosecutor's words of a five-million-dollar fine and thirty years in prison rang in his ears. By the time he got out of prison, he would be sixty-two. His dream of being a dad was being stolen from him before it had even begun.

The flight attendant reminds him to put his seat up, and soon the plane is descending through the clouds, returning to the real world. The plane touches down so gently, the sleeping baby across the aisle doesn't wake.

As soon as the plane lands in Rochester, New York, Zach heads to the car rental desk where Scott had reserved a car for him. He sets the GPS to Pine Lake — estimated travel time, about two hours. *Not long enough*, he thinks, putting the car into drive.

It is late May, but in the mountains midday temperatures barely climb out of the 50s. The trees and flowers are just green and have yet to bloom.

He exits the highway, turns onto Mountainview Road, and drives through town. With school still in session, tourist season hasn't started, and everything is still quiet.

He pulls into the Pine View Inn, seeing only two other cars in the parking lot. He parks the car and unfolds his stiff body, sore from the flight and the drive in the subcompact car, and stretches his legs before heading inside for a room.

At the front desk is a woman, her brown curly hair falling just below her shoulders and freckles dotting her round cheeks. Warmth seems to flow from her as she bends down, offering a hug to a young girl, carefully wiping her tears and whispering something to soothe her. The girl giggles. Her matching curls bounce on her head, identifying her as the woman's child.

"This is my daughter Emma," she says and without missing a beat, the woman smiles and turns her attention to him.

"Can I help you?"

He's startled, having lost himself in the moment.

"How can I help you?" she asks again, smiling.

"Oh, yeah. I would like a room," Zach says.

The little girl is playing with a toy boat, pretending her mermaid is sailing it as her mom types away at the keyboard, making the reservation.

"Do you like sailing?" Zach asks the little girl, pointing to her toy boat.

"It's not a sailboat," she says. "It's my pirate ship."

"How many nights?" the woman asks.

"I guess one," Zach says.

"Okay, I will just need your ID and your credit card."

Zach hands her his driver's license and American Express Black Card.

"Hartmann? You must be Blake Hartmann's son," she says as she runs his card.

"Something like that," Zach says, not wanting to be associated with his father.

Her nametag reads "Missy Wagner," and underneath, he sees that her title is general manager. She looks less than thirty—very young to be in charge of a hotel, even a small country inn like this.

"What are you doing staying here and not with your dad? He's going to be so excited to see you."

"I guess," Zach says, just wanting the conversation to end.

"Actually, there seems to be an issue with your card."

"What?" Zach asks, his face flushed.

"I'm sorry, but it didn't go through."

"You've got to be kidding me!" Zach says. He thought he would at least have a few days before the banks received the court order to freeze his assets. Zach reaches to turn her computer monitor. In his rush, his elbow hits her pink mug, spilling her coffee on her lilac-colored dress.

She jolts backward and gasps.

"Oh my goodness, I'm so sorry," Zach says, flustered.

Missy laughs, shaking off her surprise, and Zach smiles, feeling relaxed at its light and airy sound. "No problem. Accidents happen," she says, pulling out some napkins from under the desk to clean up the mess.

"Let me help you," Zach says, grabbing some of the napkins and starting to dab the front of her dress.

"I think I got it," Missy says, still laughing.

"Of course," Zach says, embarrassed. *What was I thinking?*

"So, do you have another card?" Missy asks.

His hand goes to the pocket of his suit jacket, thinking of the money Scott gave him. How long can he manage with just $250? He hadn't thought about how long he would stay; he'd only taken the envelope from Scott because he hadn't known what else to do. With no money and no job, he didn't have a lot of options.

"Never mind the room. Thank you anyway," Zach says, taking a deep breath and shoving the cards back into his wallet.

Turning to leave, he's still a bit dazed. *How could the freeze on his assets have taken effect so quickly?* This was a whole new league of trouble for him. Absentmindedly he pulls the door open, tripping on the sill, and the edge of the door strikes him in the middle of his forehead.

"Oh my gosh," Missy gasps. "Are you okay?"

Zach blushes and rubs the spot where the door smashed into him. "I'm fine. Hey, sorry about, well, before. It's been kind of a hard week."

Missy turns her head, stifling a giggle.

He rests his fist against the doorframe as if considering his next move. "You have a great laugh," he says, smiling back at her, then heads out to his car.

It had been a long day. Putting the key in the ignition, he leans his head back against the headrest and exhales loudly.

Isn't the trial enough? Now I have to go see my dad, too? Maybe I could just sleep in the rental car, he thinks, weighing his options before putting the car in drive.

Chapter 2

Catherine Davis dims the lights and stokes the fire in the living room fireplace. She checks the champagne, which she's put on ice, and places the champagne glasses on the coffee table, so everything is just right.

Taking one last look in the mirror, she adjusts her chest in her short black lace slip. *Is it too much?* she thinks, pulling up the top of her slip. *No, that's too little.* With that she brings back the oomph and lights some candles for ambiance.

She picks up a framed photograph from the end table and looks at the picture of Blake holding her close. She traces the curve of his scarf that he had carefully wrapped around her neck, remembering that snowy winter day and how Blake had had to coax her out onto the frozen lake. As she'd stepped onto the ice her ankles had wobbled in her skates, and she was sure she was going to fall, but she quickly found her stride and was soon gliding smoothly, hand in hand with Blake. More than two years later, she still remembers how the cold air felt on her face and how he'd brought her back to life with their first kiss as the snow fell, lightly dusting her shoulders.

Being with Blake, she felt safe again—something she had never imagined possible after losing Aleksandra the year before. She was so lost in her grief that most days she could barely breathe, much less imagine laughing or feeling giddy again. It was still painful to remember how broken she was when they'd first met. Somehow Blake's love and understanding had been like a glue that had pieced her back together. She could finally smile and laugh again, and it felt so good to be alive.

Setting the photo back down, she feels sad thinking about how much things had changed since that day. What if that isn't enough anymore?

Shortly after they'd met, she had rented out her house in the city and moved to Pine Lake full-time, to start her life with him. She doesn't want to keep doing his-and-hers houses anymore, but he seems content seeing her one or two nights a week after work. She feels alone in her fantasies of their life together, and wonders if he ever imagines them growing old together, walking the dogs at sunset, like she does.

She grabs a clip and pulls her hair up. Turning to check her reflection, she puts her hair back down and swipes on some red lipstick, then wipes it off again when her phone rings.

"You will not believe what just happened," Missy gushes on the other end. Not waiting for Catherine to respond, she continues. "The most adorable guy just came in for a room and accidentally spilled coffee all over me. Then his card was rejected, and when he tried to hightail it out of here, he walked into the front door." Missy roars with laughter at her own story.

"This is not the time, Missy," Catherine says, cutting Missy off. "I look ridiculous over here."

"Is that tonight? I totally forgot."

"Why did I listen to you about this whole seduction scene? I must have undone and redone my hair a million times."

"When he sees you half naked beside a fire, with champagne, he won't be thinking about your hair, if you know what I mean," Missy teases.

"I wouldn't be so sure about that. Things don't look the same at forty five years as they do at twenty six."

"Go make yourself a drink and just promise me you will try to have fun."

Catherine hears the door open and her heart skips a beat. "I have to go," she says hurriedly, dropping her phone, which falls under the coffee table.

Blake walks in the room, his green eyes making her heart skip a beat.

"Wow, you look amazing. What's the occasion?"

Catherine spins around for him before slipping her arms around his waist. "Thursday," she says, leading him into the living room, where she pours them each a glass of champagne. "What shall we toast to?" she asks.

"To more Thursdays," Blake teases.

"To a lifetime of Thursdays," Catherine says as they clink glasses.

"I don't know how I got so lucky," Blake whispers.

He puts his hands around her waist and gently pulls her toward him. She closes her eyes and feels his smooth lips on hers. The feeling is so familiar, it makes her melt into his arms. She's hungry for his touch as his hands slide down her back, drawing her nearer as they sink into the couch. Catherine closes her eyes, feeling at home as she rests her head on Blake's chest and listens to the beat of his heart and the crackle of the fire as a log shifts in the fireplace.

"Why do you love me?" she murmurs.

"Why do you always ask me that?" Blake asks, kissing the top of her head.

"I forget, so I need you to tell me again."

A sound makes her pull back.

"What was that?"

"Probably just the wind outside. Now, where were we?" Blake asks, nuzzling her neck.

"There it is again. You have to go check it out," Catherine pleads, patting his chest to snap him out of the moment.

Before Blake can move, they hear the front door swing open and a voice call out, "Dad?"

Blake rushes to the foyer.

"Zach, is that you? Oh my goodness, what a surprise!" Blake says, pulling his son into a tight squeeze. "Honey, it's Zach!"

"What?" Catherine calls out, furiously searching for something to cover up with. After all this time, why did Zach have to show up tonight, of all nights? As their footsteps approach, she grabs the throw blanket from the sofa in desperation.

"Come on in. You have to meet Catherine," she overhears Blake saying.

"Who?" Zach asks.

She finishes wrapping herself in an awkward toga just as Blake drags Zach in the room. His arm encircles his son's shoulders in a side hug. She softens momentarily, noticing the big, dopey smile across Blake's face. She knows how much he misses his son.

"I'm sorry—I can see that I'm interrupting. I should have called first," Zach says, his face turning red.

"No, no, it's totally fine. Isn't it, honey?" Blake asks.

"Don't apologize! We are so glad you're here," Catherine says, offering a warm smile. Clutching her blanket to stay covered, her eyes dart around the room, trying to figure out how to sneak past them and get dressed.

"Come have a seat," Blake says, patting the cushion next to him on the love seat, inviting Zach to sit down. "Can I get you something to drink? Champagne, or maybe a beer?" Blake asks.

"A beer would be great," Zach says.

"You two catch up for a moment. I need a sweater." Catherine laughs, scooting past them on her way upstairs.

She had wanted tonight to be special, just the two of them. She'd imagined a champagne-fueled conversation where he would tell her how he wanted them to move in together, ending with them curled up in each other's arms until well after the sun came up. She wants to be happy for Blake, but she can't help feeling disappointed. *Couldn't he have come any other night but this one?*

She races upstairs and slides on her jeans and a sweater before plopping down on the bed. She can't help but think back on all the special moments she had with Aleksandra, from her birth to her first steps and her first day of school. Her heart breaks, imagining how Blake must feel. He missed so many moments with Zach that he can't ever get back. Under his smile she can see the sadness and longing etched in his face.

She fixes her sweater and turns to check her hair in the mirror before heading back downstairs.

Zach stands as Catherine comes in and apologizes again for interrupting.

"Don't worry about it. So, tell me, what brings you to town?" Catherine asks, sitting down on the opposite sofa and picking up her champagne glass.

"I had a client meeting nearby and thought it would be nice to visit," Zach says.

"How long has it been since you were last here? Three years?" Blake asks patting Zach on the back.

"Ten years, Dad," Zach mutters, absentmindedly peeling the label off his beer bottle.

"Ten years?" Catherine asks, nearly choking on her champagne.

"Wow, that long. The years seem to go by so fast, I can't keep track," Blake says.

"How long are you in town for?" Catherine asks.

"I'm not sure, but not too long."

"You aren't sure?" Catherine questions.

"Tell me, how's your mama doing?" Blake asks.

"She's fine. I'm actually waiting on a big deal to go through. You never know how long that might take," Zach says, shifting in his seat.

Catherine leans in. "What are you working on?"

"It's been a long day and I'm feeling really tired," Zach responds, standing up. "If you don't mind, I think I'll turn in."

"You know where your room is. Get some rest, and we'll catch up in the morning," Blake calls out, but Zach has already left.

"This is quite unexpected," Catherine says, blowing out the candles.

"I know. Ten years since he's been home. This is great!"

Catherine rolls her eyes. She understands his excitement at Zach being home, but how could he go ten years and not make it a priority to see his son? *Is this how he treats the people he loves most in his life?* she wonders.

As Blake pours her another glass of champagne, he spots something underneath the coffee table. He looks closer and pulls out Catherine's phone.

"What's this doing here?" Blake laughs, and sits down next to her on the couch.

Catherine blushes. "I wondered where I put that."

"You are always in such a rush. Just slow down and pay more attention."

Catherine's eyes burn from his comment.

"I think we should take this upstairs," Blake says, rubbing her thigh.

"Behave! Zach is just down the hall."

Upstairs in bed, Catherine feels the weight of Blake's hand on her thigh as he pulls her closer to him, molding his body around hers. She relaxes into him as he places soft kisses on her shoulder. She feels the rise and fall of his chest and the rhythm of her breath as it falls into sync with his. She places her hand on his as she drifts off to sleep.

The next morning Zach wakes to the smell of bacon and eggs. He checks the time—6:30 a.m. So early. He slides on his suit pants and the button-down shirt he'd had on the day before.

He finds his father in the kitchen, wearing sweatpants and a T-shirt, a dish towel slung over his shoulder and a spatula in hand, tending the eggs on the stove.

Growing up he didn't get to spend much time with his dad, but when he did, he could count on finding him up at sunrise, cooking up a full breakfast of eggs and bacon and freshly squeezed juice. Zach smiles, thinking how funny it is that things can change so much yet stay the same.

"Sleep well?" Blake asks.

"I guess so," Zach says, running his fingers through his hair, attempting to comb it into place.

"Looks like work is really killing you these days," Blake says, noting the dark circles under his son's eyes, and how his once-athletic build has wasted away.

"This deal is just taking a lot of my time," Zach says, sitting down at the breakfast table, avoiding eye contact.

Blake loads up a plate with two eggs over easy, bacon, and toast, and sets it down in front of Zach.

"Coffee or juice?" Blake asks.

"Both," Zach says, his mouth already full of bacon.

"Are you going to visit Grammy and Grandpa while you're in town?" Blake asks.

"I don't think it's a good time for the family reunion," Zach says blowing on his hot coffee.

Catherine walks in and pours herself a cup of coffee, kissing Blake on the cheek. He snaps his dish towel on her butt.

"That's the most action I've had in a while," she says, rolling her eyes at Blake.

"You didn't have to dress so formally for breakfast," Catherine teases. "We're pretty casual here.

"The airline lost my bag," Zach replied.

"Tell me about this deal you're working on," Catherine says, pulling out a chair and sitting across the table from Zach. "I love talking shop."

"Catherine's a CPA," Blake says proudly. "She's negotiated some big deals. Honey, tell him about the deal you did with Jim last Christmas."

Catherine blushes. "It was just a small tech merger with a client of mine."

"You know a lot about Mergers and Acquisitions," Zach asks.

"A bit. What are you working on?"

Zach pauses, wondering how much to share with Catherine. He takes a breath and looks up, as if the answer to how much he should share with her is painted on the ceiling. Should he tell her how he got played by a manipulative and greedy man, intent on making his fortune by defrauding innocent investors out of hundreds of millions of dollars? How he got stuck holding the bag, and may spend the rest of his life in prison?

Zach decides to spare her the sob story and settles on a lighter version of the truth.

"A national food conglomerate acquired my client, who is revolutionizing the frozen food industry with their kid-friendly organic dinner kits. Moms love them."

"So, the deal already closed?" Catherine asks.

"Kind of. It's complicated," Zach says.

"What do you mean?" Catherine asks.

When he doesn't respond, she crosses and uncrosses her legs, watching as Zach stirs his black coffee, avoiding her gaze.

Zach wishes he could lay it all out there on the table. Catherine is so easy to talk to; he's tempted to tell this woman he hardly knows everything that really happened. He wants to tell her how he feels like a fool. For God's sake, he graduated top of his class with an MBA— how could he have missed all the red flags in this deal?

But if he's honest with himself, he knows he didn't miss them. Maybe that's what he is most ashamed of. He knew things weren't right. He was just too much of a coward to confront Mr. Anderson and put a stop to his deception. Zach had done dozens of deals with Mr. Anderson over the ten years they'd worked together, so he had noticed things were different with this deal. Mr. Anderson was being secretive, leaving Zach out of calls and meetings, and handling the audit on his own. Nonetheless, Zach had wanted his commission, so he'd turned a blind eye. When did he become the guy who abandons his principles for a commission?

"I think I'll go shower," Zach says, turning to leave.

"I guess you liked it," Blake says as he scoops up Zach's empty dishes from the table and begins washing up.

"Thanks for breakfast," Zach says patting his dad on the back.

"I'm heading over to the Pine View Inn to set up their docks. Why don't you join me? After, we can head into town and grab a few things for you, until they find your bags," Blake suggests to Zach.

Zach pushes his hands into his pockets, trying to think of an excuse to skip the father–son bonding activity, but with nothing on his schedule, he just says, "Sure, sounds great."

"You can grab a T-shirt and jeans from my closet," Blake says.

"Dad jeans. Great," Zach says, shaking his head as he heads upstairs to shower.

Blake dries his hands on the dish towel and slides in next to Catherine at the table.

"Maybe a rain check on last night when I get back?" Blake winks, brushing his nose against her cheek.

Catherine doesn't take the bait. "So, how much do you know about his business deal?"

Blake picks up her mug and refills her coffee, setting it back down in front of her.

"No more than what he just shared. Why?"

After taking a sip, Catherine says, "It just seems strange, don't you think?"

"He seems to be working hard on this deal. I'm sure he's just tired or stressed," Blake responds. "What's all this about?"

"If the deal is done, the contract would have outlined a timeline for transition. How would he not know how long it's going to take?" she asks. "He's not telling us something."

"Why are you making a big deal out of this? You're acting like some sort of detective," Blake says, reaching for her hand across the table.

"I just think he was acting strange. Aren't you worried about him?"

"Strange? You haven't even known him for twelve hours," Blake says.

"For example, if he has a client nearby, why is this the first time he's come for a visit in ten years?"

"Look, all that matters right now is that he's here. Why can't you just be happy for me instead of trying to make this some kind of conspiracy?"

"Because something is not right. Call it a mother's intuition."

"He's my son. I think I know him better than you do."

"Got it. My opinion doesn't matter."

"Now you're twisting my words and making this all about you."

"I'm just wondering why you don't find it strange that your son, who hasn't been home in a decade, shows up randomly without a phone call, or a bag."

22

"I'm his dad. He doesn't need to call."

Catherine pinches the bridge of her nose, then rubs her forehead and sighs.

Blake shoves his chair back and slams his coffee mug on the granite counter. "This is my son and you don't know him, so just stay out of it."

"When you don't like what I have to say, you just shut down the conversation. How does that even work in a relationship?" Catherine asks.

"I gave you the emotional space you needed when you were grieving Aleksandra."

"How dare you even compare the two? You're not grieving!" Catherine says, standing up to go.

She's almost out the door when she spins around, frustrated. "Don't forget dinner with my parents tomorrow night."

Blake doesn't answer. He waves a hand, acknowledging her comment, then returns to his washing up.

Chapter 3

Every year the Pine View Inn welcomes the summer season on Memorial Day weekend with their Slice of Summer Picnic. Granddaddy and Ya-Ya had started this tradition when they opened the Inn sixty-five years ago. With Granddaddy's passing in January, Missy was determined to make this year's picnic the best ever, in his honor.

She had spent every summer of her childhood at the lake with her grandparents. Back then the Inn was always buzzing with the regular guests, in town for their summer vacation. Missy would wake up early and help Granddaddy raise the flag and hang red, white, and blue bunting on the freshly painted white deck railings while Ya-Ya would water her hanging baskets of pink and purple petunias.

By lunchtime, the games would start, with a pie-eating contest and a balloon toss on the back lawn. As the sun rose high in the sky, the kids would head down to the lake for the swimming competition. The lifeguard grouped the kids by age and blew a whistle to signal the start of the race.

Missy would run through the warm sand into the lake and paddle as fast as she could to the rope at the edge of the swimming section and then turn around and paddle back to shore. Smiling and shivering, she'd emerge from the ice-cold water and collected her blue ribbon from the lifeguard. Grabbing her towel from the sand, she would race to the patio and wait in line to get a hot dog from Granddaddy and some cold lemonade pie from Ya-Ya. All the kids would sit together in the grass and eat their lunch.

At sunset, some adults would take out the Inn's green canoes for a paddle around the cove while others would relax on the covered deck. As darkness set in, the kids would run around the lawn catching fireflies and Granddaddy would build a fire so they could roast marshmallows.

Granddaddy and Ya-Ya were always the heart and soul of the Inn, but now, look at this place, Missy thinks to herself, picking flaking paint off the rotting deck railings. *How did this happen, when Granddaddy had always been so meticulous about repairs and maintenance?* If she was truly honest with herself, however, she had noticed that he'd let things slide in recent years. He had slowed down and was more tired.

Stepping back inside, she notices a new water stain on the main room ceiling and adds it to her mental list of repairs needed. *I guess I should have taken on more of the responsibility*, she thinks. *I should have noticed how tired Granddaddy was and stepped up so he could have retired. I should have picked up the slack for him.*

This past year had been even harder on Ya-Ya. After losing Granddaddy back in January, Ya-Ya was heartbroken. Then pneumonia had landed her in the hospital for over a month. Missy worries that at eighty-five, this might be too much for her.

The thought of losing Ya-Ya terrifies Missy. She's more than just her grandmother; she's been like a second mother to her, and to Emma. During those stormy months in college when she got pregnant, there'd been a major rupture with her parents. Her mom and dad thought she should just put Emma up for adoption, so she could focus on her education and "put her mistakes in her past."

Thankfully, Ya-Ya loves her unconditionally, and she and Granddaddy had taken her in, with the new baby. From the moment Emma was born, Ya-Ya had been by her side. Being a single mom isn't easy, but Ya-Ya made it easier, helping out at three a.m. when Emma wouldn't stop crying as an infant, or giving her a warm hug after a long day of toddler tantrums.

Even now, when Emma is four—or "four and three-quarters," as Emma would remind her—she is so grateful when Ya-Ya makes dinner so Missy can work late on paperwork, or when she teaches Emma the names of the birds at the feeder while they share an afternoon snack. *What would I do without her?*

She can hear them now in the kitchen, playing while they do the dishes.

Settling down at her desk, Missy notices the silence in the hotel, a fact that makes her even more depressed. *I don't think I can do this without you*, Missy says, like a prayer to Granddaddy, while poring over the ledgers piled on the desk in front of her. She doesn't know why he still used paper ledger books to track the income and expenses of the Inn, but she feels overwhelmed trying to make sense of them.

Once she had some time, she was definitely going to computerize things and take advantage of one of the apps or software programs Catherine kept mentioning. How she does this for a living, Missy will never understand. She feels dizzy sorting the receipts and logging them into columns. Of course, Catherine had offered to help her many times, but Missy doesn't want to take advantage. They are close friends, and Catherine probably just offers to be nice.

27

The phone rings and Missy grabs it, anxious for a distraction.

"Have you been outside yet today? It's beautiful! I was hoping I could coax you out for coffee or lunch out on the deck?" Catherine says.

"God, I haven't. I'm too busy having a small panic attack about my mile-long to-do list before we open this weekend. It's not just the guests, but Channel 8 News is covering the picnic," Missy says, looking at the reports on her desk and then out the window at the sunshine and clear blue skies.

Although Missy feels guilty about leaving her desk, she eventually accepts Catherine's offer. It's just too tempting, and she knows she needs the break.

An hour later, when Catherine walks through the door, she can see from Missy's expression that things aren't good. She walks up to meet her behind the front desk, pulling Missy into a big hug.

"Something's gotta give," Missy sighs. "I'm counting on the Slice of Summer Picnic. This has to work."

"Sounds like my day," Catherine says hopping up on the desk, "I thought I could take some photos for you to post on social media," she says, and reaches into her bag and pulls out her camera .

"Ya-Ya just made your favorite lemonade pie. Have a slice with me," Missy says.

"What are you doing, letting Ya-Ya make pies at her age?" Catherine asks.

"Like I could stop her. You know how she is."

Missy leads her through the hotel lobby, passing the common area, which feels warm and cozy with a small fire burning in the two-story stone fireplace. Sun streams through the floor-to-ceiling windows onto the leather couches, which offer a great view of the lake.

Missy pops into the restaurant and orders two iced teas before they head out onto the back deck, overlooking the water.

Catherine closes her eyes, feeling the sun on her face. The trees aren't in bloom yet, but she can feel summer coming.

"Fresh from the icebox," Ya-Ya says, swinging through the door with Emma on her heels.

Missy jumps up and takes the tray from Ya-Ya. "What are you doing, carrying this out here?"

"I made it with love, so I know it will make you all better," Ya-Ya says with a wink.

"She still won't share her secret recipe with anyone," Missy tells Catherine.

When she dies, her lemonade pie will die with her, Missy thinks. *When Emma is my age, she may not even remember the magic of it.*

"Arrgghh, matey," Emma says.

"Are we under attack?" Catherine asks, laughing at Emma in her pirate costume.

"Do you have any golden treasure?" Emma asks.

"We just wanted to come and say hello," Ya-Ya says, hugging Catherine and kissing her on the cheek, leaving a red imprint from her lipstick.

"Come on, Ya-Ya, let's go find the treasure," Emma says, pulling her by the hand back toward the kitchen.

Ya-Ya had been baking her lemonade pie for longer than Missy has been alive.

Missy remembers a time when she was seven, playing on the swings in the backyard with a group of summer kids—what they called the kids who were around during the tourist season. The biggest one, Billy, dared Missy to jump off the swing after going as high as she could. She did, and scraped both knees when she landed. Ya-Ya rushed over and scooped her up. After she cleaned off the blood, she gave Missy a big piece of her lemonade pie. Over the years there had been many scary, difficult—and celebratory—moments punctuated by this dessert.

Missy sighs and puts her fork down. "I hope the publicity from the picnic boosts my reservations."

"Still slow?" Catherine asks.

Missy nods. "It wasn't always like this; I just don't know what to do."

"How can your hotel be such a well-kept secret?"

"I mean, look at this place. The wallpaper is outdated, the carpets are threadbare, the paint is peeling, and the roof is leaking. How am I supposed to fix all of this with reservations down? On top of that, the bank called and said they won't extend our line of credit."

"It will get better," Catherine says and reaches across the table and gives Missy's hand a gentle squeeze.

"Easy for you to say as you enjoy life in your beautiful home with your beautiful horses on five acres," Missy snaps

"Easy?" Catherine snorts and her eyes water as she thinks how she would trade every dollar she has to spend another day with her daughter.

"I'm so sorry, I didn't mean that. Missy quickly apologizes. I don't even know how I can keep the Inn open if we have another bad season," Missy says, pushing her pie around her plate and thinking about the new Traveler's Inn Motel just down the street. It opened last season as a discount motel, flaunting its rooms for $49 a night. She hadn't thought it would hurt her business this badly. She'd believed that her guests would still want the personalized experience her Inn offered, but she was afraid she'd underestimated how many of her guests preferred the discount available at the Traveler's Inn.

"Trust me, I understand," Catherine offers. "I was exactly your age when I bought that house. My business was just starting, Aleksandra was a baby, and my budget was stretched thin."

She pauses thinking back to how her life has changed since she was twenty-six and just starting out in life. She worked hard to juggle being a mom and to build her business. At work, her efforts paid off as her accounting firm grew to twenty five partners. At home, she scrimped and saved and was able to buy a nice home in the city in addition to her home in Pine Lake. As Aleksandra got older, Catherine was able to give her riding lessons and eventually her first horse Breezy and later her second horse Tinka. Her life may look easy as she hadn't worked as much since losing Aleksandra three years ago, but it was anything but. "Fewer reservations means less money, which means less cash for renovations. It's a vicious cycle. And look at this review," Missy says, opening her phone and pulling up the latest online review.

"This hotel feels very old and outdated and in need of a major renovation. Would not stay here again. But the rooms were clean, the food was good, and the staff was very nice," Catherine reads aloud. "See, they had some nice things to say," she says, trying to comfort her friend.

"And what if something happens to Ya-Ya," Missy says, brushing a tear from her eye. "It's all just too much," she says.

"You're being too hard on yourself," Catherine says, taking another bite of pie.

Missy is quiet, taking in the wide back lawn and dark blue water, reflecting the fluffy white clouds dotting the sky, thinking about how some people would give anything to trade places with her and live on the lake.

"Life sure is funny. I never saw myself living in Pine Lake, much less running my grandparents' Inn."

"I know. I didn't see myself living here, either," Catherine agrees.

"I just don't know how they did it. Granddaddy and Ya-Ya always had it together, checking everything off their list of projects, from weeding the gardens to staining the deck, or patching the roof. I'm not sure I'm cut out for this."

Catherine puts her fork down and covers Missy's hand with her own. "They didn't try to do it all on their own. When are you going to let someone help you? Blake said he'd do the renovations at cost, and I told you I can help you with the books," Catherine suggests.

Missy ignores her comments, and continues.

"Back then, their customers always booked their reservation for the next summer before they'd even loaded up their station wagons. Ya-Ya even had to keep a waiting list, while I can't even fill the Inn. I just feel like I am letting them down," Missy moans.

31

Catherine breathes in the scent of fresh lavender, in its first bloom of the season.

"This spot is so gorgeous. I know things are going to get better for you!"

Missy agrees, and her mood lightens for the moment.

"You know, that lavender blooms again in July, and the garden is full of butterflies. It would make the perfect backdrop for a summer wedding," she teases.

"Let's not get ahead of ourselves. I don't even have a ring, and at this rate, I'm not sure I'll ever get one," Catherine complains.

Marriage had never been a priority for Catherine. She'd had her accounting firm and Aleksandra, and her life was full. But now with Aleksandra gone, it feels different. She wants more with Blake.

Missy waves her words away.

"The ceremony could be right over there, in front of the garden. We could transform the lawn for an elegant sunset reception—lights everywhere, round tables for dinner, soft music playing. You and Blake could have your first dance right there, by the water."

Catherine can see the pictures Missy is painting in her mind's eye, and for a moment she can imagine herself laughing with the guests and dancing to the band, playing their song.

"Sounds beautiful, but Blake isn't there yet, and I don't know that he ever will be. I mean, I rented out my home in the city and moved here. I have rearranged my entire life to be with him."

"He loves you," Missy says. "Just give him time."

"How much time does he need? I want to be with someone who wakes up excited to be with me, who knows how lucky he is, and is actually ready to spend forever with me. Is that too much to ask?"

"I've seen how he looks at you. He'll get there," Missy reassures her.

"I'm not so sure anymore. It's already been over two years," Catherine whines. "Oh, and I didn't even tell you that after I set up that whole romantic evening, his son walked in out of the blue. He hasn't been home in years, and he chooses last night to stop by for a visit," she continues, without stopping for a breath.

"Blake must be so happy."

"I guess," Catherine sighs. "Apparently Zach is here working on a business deal." Catherine pauses, surprised by the tears threatening to roll down her cheeks. Taking a deep breath, she continues. "There's just always something distracting him from us."

"You know Blake loves you," Missy says.

"I promised myself I would never relocate for a man. Now look at me. What am I doing?" Catherine asks.

Missy gives her a playful shove.

"I know. I run my business and I raised my daughter, but now this man has me falling apart and questioning everything all the time. What's wrong with me?" Catherine laughs at herself.

"You can't be perfect at everything," Missy teases.

The receptionist comes over to their table, calling Missy back to work.

"I'm sorry, duty calls," Missy says, and heads back to work.

Suddenly by herself again, Catherine looks out over the lake. She slips off her flip-flops and walks across the back lawn to the water's edge. Rolling up her jeans, she wades into the shallow water, feeling the water lap across her toes. Off to her right she sees a dragonfly sunning itself on top of a cattail.

She quietly moves closer so as not to disturb it and slowly raises her camera. Adjusting the focus and angle, she snaps a few shots before it is startled. She watches it fly away and smiles. Her eyes well up with sudden tears, thinking of how Aleksandra would have teased her for taking more dragonfly pictures. Not a day goes by that she doesn't think about Aleksandra. *I wish you were here right now*, she thinks, as the water ripples around her ankles.

Chapter 4

a few hours later, Blake and Zach pull into the parking lot outside the Inn. Before they begin the arduous task of placing the floating docks into the lake for the season, Zach takes a moment to notice the serene blue sky. Zach's mom, Jenny, moved away from Pine Lake to Minnesota when she was pregnant with Zach, and she still reminisced with him often about the unique and perfect shade of blue of the Pine Lake sky that faded seamlessly into the placid water. After traveling to -three countries, Zach has to agree there wasn't anywhere that matched the peaceful sky blending into the earth like Pine Lake.

Zach had never understood what his mom saw in his dad, but he knows she was devastated to leave Blake and Pine Lake behind when she moved to Minnesota with her parents. When she'd found out she was pregnant, his parents had agreed it was best for her to go and live with her folks, so they could help her when the baby was born. She gave up love, college, and her hopes and dreams, all to take care of him, but what had his dad ever done for him? Sent a card on his birthday and Christmas? He'd watched his friends head off to father–son camping trips and learn important skills, like how to change the oil in a car or work on a lawn mower. Sometimes they would invite him along, but it wasn't the same. What kind of dad can't be bothered to make time for his kid's games or graduations or any of the million moments that make up a life?

The summer Zach turned seventeen, his mother had finally lost her patience with his skipping classes and wild partying every weekend and sent him to Pine Lake to live with his dad. For some kids, this may have been a reason to celebrate, but for Zach, who hadn't spent more than a day or two with his dad since he was born, it felt like a jail sentence. All his friends were going out and partying together all summer while he was stuck living in a sleepy, remote town halfway across the country from them, and working full-time at the Pine Lake Marina.

Every single morning, he was up before the sun, filling the rental boats with gas and getting them ready for tourists. He spent his days teaching them how to operate the boats and giving waterskiing lessons to their kids. He worked late into the night, wiping down the boats and making sure they were ready for the next day. By the time the weekend came, his muscles ached and he just wanted to sleep, but he made the best tips on the weekends, so he worked all day Saturday and Sunday. It was hard work, but Zach grew to love his time on the water. While Zach now faced bigger issues than he'd faced when he was seventeen, he still couldn't help hoping he'd have a few days this summer to enjoy being out on the water.

He pulls his hat down over his eyes as they head to the Inn, hoping Missy won't notice him after the scene he made yesterday.

"Hey, Missy, Catherine said you could use a hand with your docks, so I'm going to pull my truck around back and get started," Blake says.

"Sounds good—I'll meet you back there," Missy replies, coming out from behind the front desk. "I don't think we formally introduced ourselves when you stopped in yesterday. I'm Missy," she says, holding out her hand to Zach.

Zach shakes her hand in silence and nods his head.

"You two know each other?" Blake asks.

"We spoke when he stopped in yesterday, looking for a room," Missy says.

"You were going to stay at the Inn?" Blake asks, his brows furrowed. He stares at Zach as if looking at a stranger.

"Have you decided how long you're going to stay in town?" Missy asks.

Zach, usually articulate, stammers, trying to think of a reply, when Emma came skipping through the lobby, swinging her baby doll and singing, "Yo-ho, I have gold in me chest, yo-ho."

Blake bends down to scoop up Emma and twirl her around. "Hey, kiddo! How's my favorite pirate?" he asks, before setting Emma back down and ruffling her hair.

Zach stifles a laugh, thankful she's lightened the mood.

"Gary, from the marina, always used to put my docks in for the season, but he retired last fall," Missy says, getting back to business.

"You know Catherine and I are always happy to lend a hand," Blake reassures her. Blake bends down and scoops up Emma and twirls her around. "Hey kiddo," Blake says. "How's my favorite pirate?" he asks Emma setting her back down and ruffling her hair.

"Thank you! We are so lucky to have you. You're a lifesaver," Missy says, wrapping Blake in a big hug.

"At least someone thinks so," Zach mutters under his breath.

"I really didn't know what to do, with all the guests coming in for the season this weekend. A few have asked whether there would be a place to tie up their boat. I had no idea how I would have things ready in time."

"It's a good excuse for me to drop off these updated designs for the renovation," Blake says.

Missy's stomach lurches as she looks at the designs. She knows everything he's suggested is more than necessary; what she doesn't know is how she can possibly afford it.

"Well, I better get back and leave you two to your work. There's so much to be done!"

"Let me know what you think," Blake calls out.

"Uh-huh," Missy responds, stumbling back toward the lobby while paging through the printout of his suggested upgrades.

Blake surveys the back lawn where the fragmented floating dock sections were stored for the winter, developing his strategy to move them into the lake.

"Okay son, it looks like the straightest path is to—"

Zach holds up his hand, cutting him off.

"I spent an entire summer dropping docks in. I think I've got it."

"You have to be really careful—the sections can have a mind of their own. If you push too hard, you'll tear up the whole landscape. You've got to guide them gently and ease them in."

"Whatever," Zach grumbles.

"You drive and I'll guide you. Keep it nice and slow," Blake says.

Zach hops into the truck and rolls down the driver and passenger windows to hear his dad's instructions. After they hook the first section up, he puts the truck into drive and drags it toward the lake.

"Turn the wheel more to the right. Now straighten up," Blake says.

Zach puts the truck in park and hops out to position the floating dock section. Taking off his shoes and rolling up his jeans, he slowly wades into the water. Gasping as the icy water laps against his calves, he secures the first dock section and heads back to shore to move the next dock section into place.

"So, what's the deal with you and Catherine?" Zach asks, holding the next dock section in place while Blake sets the posts.

"What can I say? She's something else."

"Is it serious?" Zach asks.

"She lost her daughter, Aleksandra, in an accident a few years back, and it nearly broke her. She's had a really rough time, but she's found her way through. Once you get to know her, you will see how gentle and loving she is," Blake says.

"So, are you going to settle down—make things permanent?"

"I think things are just fine the way they are," Blake says, checking that the dock section is secured.

"That's the way it always is with you, isn't it? Always aloof. Everything is fine."

"Like I said, push too hard and you can tear up the whole damn landscape. Believe me, I speak from experience."

Zach scrunches his forehead, not quite understanding. Was there more to the story than he realized?

"What about you? Anyone special back home?" Blake asks as they hook the third dock section to the truck.

Zach thinks about Tracey, how they have been seeing each other on and off for more than seven years.

"No one serious," he says, hopping back in the truck.

"You need to drag this section exactly three feet to the right so we can easily place the last one right here," Blake says.

"I know. I got it," Zach says, rolling his eyes.

"Just don't go too far left," Blake reminds him.

Zach helps Blake unhook the last section from the truck and slide it into the lake. After setting the final post to secure the entire dock, they admire their work.

"This was nice, wasn't it?" Blake asks, patting Zach on the back.

Zach slides his hands in his pockets, exhaling. He realizes it felt good to be working outside, with the sun on his face and the breeze blowing through his hair.

"I think I'm going to stay here a little while longer," Zach says to his dad, not quite ready to leave.

Zach waves as his dad hops in the truck and drives slowly across the back lawn, heading home. He returns his gaze to the quiet lake. The late afternoon sun is high in the sky, and without boat traffic, the water is as smooth as glass. The mountains are reflected in its surface like a mirror.

He feels seventeen all over again, especially because things with his dad never seem to change. It's like he still sees him as that immature wild kid who toilet-papered the neighbors' trees and snuck out after midnight to go drinking at Pine Lake State Park. Even though he grew up and finished college, got his MBA, and made something of himself, his dad only notices his shortcomings and mistakes. Zach thinks about all the biting words he wishes he could spew at his dad, but doesn't. He doesn't have the energy to fight—and what would it change anyway?

Sighing deeply, he realizes he hasn't thought about the trial all day. *How did I get so lost?* he wonders. *What if I spend the next thirty years of my life in prison without breathing this fresh mountain air or watching the sun's reflection in the water as it dips behind the mountains? What if I've wasted years of my life chasing the next big deal and I never really have a chance to fall in love or have a family? What if I have worked so hard for nothing, when all of this was right here the whole time?*

He peels off his shirt and dives into the cold lake water, washing away all the stress and tension.

"Looks amazing," Missy calls out as she approaches the dock with a tray holding two iced teas.

Zach helps himself to a glass and looks over to the swimming area he and his dad had just set the ropes for, thinking how the beach and swimming area look exactly the same today as it did when he was a teenager. The white lifeguard stand is perched on the fresh sand overlooking the water, ready to protect this summer's group of swimmers, just where it always was.

His cousin had been the Inn's lifeguard that summer he spent in Pine Lake, and Zach had filled in for him a few times. He remembers one particularly hot day, being perched up in that chair. It was a busy weekend near the end of summer, and families dotted the beach. Kids were building sandcastles, parents were relaxing in their lounge chairs, reading and talking, and a large group of kids were playing a game of tag in the lake. Most of the kids in the game were older, but there was one young girl, maybe ten or eleven , trying to keep up.

As he watched the game, it was an older boy's turn to be "it." The boy turned around, closed his eyes, and counted to ten while treading water. As he counted, the swimmers darted and scattered throughout the swimming area, trying to get as far away as possible. The little girl started dog-paddling toward the deep end of the swimming area, and when the boy tuned around to give chase, he spotted her as his target and raced toward her.

The girl's legs were kicking and her arms were shoveling the water out of the way, but the older boy was catching up to her. She was trying to reach the rope at the outer edge of the swimming area, which was base, and she was almost there when her head ducked below the water.

Zach stood up in his chair and was relieved to see her pop back up and keep paddling. He watched her stretch her arms out, trying to grab the rope, and her head went under again.

He grabbed the rescue tube, hopped down from the stand, blowing his whistle for backup, and yelled at the swimmers to clear the water. He ran to the lake and dove headfirst into the water, racing toward the little girl. He grabbed her around the chest, looped the rescue tube around her, and swam back to shore. Back on the sand, she coughed up the water she had swallowed. She was still breathing, and doing okay.

Zach realizes Missy has asked him a question, but he didn't hear it.

"Sorry. I was distracted, thinking about a rescue I did when I was lifeguarding here as a teenager."

"I almost drowned in the lake one summer," Missy says.

After comparing stories, Zach realizes it was Missy he had pulled out of the lake all those years ago.

"So that was really you?" Zach smiles.

"I think it was."

"I also remember that your grandmother gave me a delicious slice of pie as a reward for saving you," Zach teases.

"She thinks that pie is the solution to everything." Missy laughs.

"Maybe she's right. It's been over twenty years, and I still remember how good it was."

"I see what you're doing here, but you're barking up the wrong tree. She is the keeper of the pie."

Zach laughs at how easily Missy is able to put him in his place.

"That's too bad. Maybe it's time for you to take on the family pie tradition," Zach suggests.

"I wish. I can't help you with the pie, but I can offer you dinner as a thank-you."

"I'd like that."

"Then it's settled. We'll have dinner here."

"I just need to wash up," Zach says, wiping his hands on his jeans.

Zach heads through the common room and down a hallway to the bathroom. The hallway is lined with photos from each year's Slice of Summer Picnic. Zach looks at an old photo of a father–son duo. Moving in closer, he sees that the little boy is smiling, the father looking down at him, his arm wrapped around his shoulders. Anyone could see the pride and love between the pair.

Zach had forgotten about the year he and his dad had won the fishing tournament. Looking at the year below the photo, he estimates he was seven years old at the time.

How did I forget this moment? he wonders. If he'd erased this memory, how many other moments had he forgotten from the times he'd shared with his dad?

Missy settles into a table on the deck, watching as the sun begins to dip below the mountains, painting the sky in shades of pink.

She can't deny Zach is handsome, with his broad shoulders and green eyes. Her stomach is full of butterflies. He is appealing and quick with a smile—she's sure he's charmed plenty of women in the city. But he also seems gentle and honest.

When she was younger, she would have enjoyed some harmless flirting with such an attractive stranger. It would have even felt exhilarating. However, she has Emma to think about now. She can't play around. If her mom were here, she would remind Missy that that's how she ended up with Emma in the first place. She has to be sensible and think about her future.

That night, as the stars begin to speckle the sky, Missy and Zach have the deck to themselves. As the server pours their water, Missy watches Zach across the table. When he'd stopped at the Inn yesterday, he had looked tired and stressed, with dark circles under his eyes, but now, even in the candlelight, Missy can see that Pine Lake is already breathing life back into him. She sees a hint of color on his face and a sparkle in his eyes.

He catches her looking at him and she hopes the darkness will hide her blush.

As their server heads off to put in their order, Missy leans close, as if sharing a secret.

"Okay, tell me the truth—what's going on?"

"What do you mean?" Zach asks.

"You're hiding from something."

"There isn't really anything to tell."

"I have been trying to figure out why you just showed up at the Inn, after all these years, in your perfectly tailored suit, with a limitless credit card that was declined."

"Why are you being so hard on me," Zach says, trying to deflect her questions.

"You can trust me. My life isn't perfect either. I just think you are hiding from something, here in Pine Lake."

"What makes you think I'm hiding?" Zach asks, intrigued by the surprising intimacy of the question.

"It seems to be what everyone comes here to do," Missy says with a smile.

"Well, not me. I'm just here visiting my dad."

"I think we both know that isn't true. Now are you going to tell me, or do I have to play detective?"

Zach is fiddling with his napkin when the server delivers the breadbasket. He grabs a dinner roll and slathers it with butter, taking a bite, to stall.

"I'm having some problems at work and I'm not sure what I'm going to do next," Zach says cautiously.

Missy nods, urging him to go on.

Zach leans back in his chair, thinking about how much he wants to share.

"I haven't told anyone about this yet, but I was involved in a business deal that went bad. I feel so stupid."

Missy gently places her hand on his.

"Things got out of hand very quickly. I hardly understand it myself."

"I don't know much about making deals, but I'm a good listener," she says.

Zach takes another bite of his roll.

"There was this guy, Bill Anderson. He seemed to have a lifestyle I'd never even dreamed of. When he hired me on and brought me into his inner circle right after college, I felt like I belonged, and that I was good enough. Maybe that seems silly, but after years of trying to get my dad to notice me, it felt good to have a boss care and mentor me. My career took off, and soon I was the guy everyone wanted a meeting with."

Missy nods, giving him her full attention.

"Turns out, he was just using me. I feel like a teenager that fell in with the wrong crowd. Do you think that can happen to adults?"

Missy blushes. "Of course I do. Some people think that about me," she says.

Zach raises an eyebrow. "I doubt that. You're here taking care of Emma and your grandmother and running the Inn."

"So, what happened with Bill Anderson?" Missy asks.

"I dunno."

"You're lying," she prods.

He was taken aback by how quick she was. It was if she'd already known him for years, and she was so easy to talk to. Like she already knew the truth and didn't judge him one bit.

"I think he may have played me and the investors in a fraudulent deal, then fled the country. Now my career is ruined. I feel like my life is over. And what do I have to show for it?"

They sit in silence as their dinner is served.

Zach cuts off a piece of his steak, savoring the bite.

"I thought maybe I would stay here a while to sort things out," Zach continues.

Missy smiles and says, "I think you are in the right place for that."

"So, what are you hiding from?" Zach says.

"Well, as long as we're being honest . . . I found out I was pregnant after my junior year of college. I was studying hospitality business management, and my parents were furious with the news. They suggested I give the baby up for adoption, but that wasn't an option for me, so I came here and helped my grandparents with the Inn and they helped me with Emma, while I finished school."

"Where's her dad?" Zach asks.

"Colorado? California, maybe? I don't know. I can't keep track anymore, and we rarely hear from him," Missy says. "How have I been friends with Blake and never met you?"

"I grew up with my mom in Minnesota. He wasn't around a lot when I was growing up. He was always working, so we aren't that close," Zach says, pensively moving the vegetables in his salad around before taking another bite.

"You're still pretty lucky, though. I would love to have parents that love me like your dad loves you."

Zach snorts. "That seems to be the consensus around here, but that wasn't my experience."

"What do you mean?"

"He worked hard and sent my mom money, but he was always too busy for me. He never understood that I just wanted my dad." Zach sighs loudly and looks out over the lake. "Never mind. It doesn't matter anymore," Zach says.

Missy reaches for his hand. "Maybe he's different now."

"Yeah, maybe," Zach agrees, smiling at her across the table.

Missy was about to respond when Emma's squeals surprised her from behind.

"Mama!" Emma calls, as she bounces out the back door and onto the deck, wearing her pajamas, Ya-Ya following behind.

Missy pushes her chair back from the table and scoops her up, setting her on her lap.

"You remember Mr. Zach?" Missy asks, prompting Emma to say hello.

"Arrgghh," Emma says.

"Ahoy, matey," Zach replies, laughing.

Emma hands a little drawing to Zach. It has three stick figures standing in front of the lake, and a rainbow. Zach thanks Emma for the picture as Ya-Ya takes Emma's hand, saying, "I think it's time for this pirate to get some sleep."

Emma, not happy about bedtime, slinks off Missy lap with slumped shoulders.

"Nice night tonight, and a new moon. Perfect for stargazing on the docks, don't you think?" Ya-Ya suggests, winking at Missy.

"I have to get going," Zach says, checking the time on his cell phone while pushing his chair back, knocking it over. Why did he suddenly feel like a clumsy teenager again?

Missy plucks his cell phone from his hand and taps a message, presumably to his father.

"There," she says, playfully tossing it back to him.

Zach bends over to pick up his chair to hide the red coming to his face.

"Come on, race you to the docks," Missy says.

"Maybe another time."

Missy kicks off her shoes and skips across the deck before racing toward the dock.

Zach hops up to follow but stops and stands frozen when he sees Missy pull her T-shirt over her head, tossing it on the lawn, and shimmy out of her jeans as she reaches the dock.

From the dock, Missy calls, "Hurry up—last one to the dock is a rotten egg!"

Zach's first impression of Missy was that she was sweet and a great listener, but this, skinny dipping under the moon was sexy. Zach follows her lead, ditching his shirt and jeans and racing to the dock. Scooping her up, he tosses her over his shoulder like a fireman and walks to the end of the dock.

"You know I could toss you in the water right now."

"You wouldn't dare!" Missy shrieks.

"Are you sure?" Zach dangles her over the water.

"No!" Missy shrieks again through a fit of giggles.

Zach sets her down gently on the dock, his hands lingering on her waist for a moment, taking in every inch of her. He gently tucks a strand of curls behind her ear, his fingers gently brushing against her cheek.

She smiles, taking his hand in hers and he feels his stomach do a flip-flop.

Still standing close, Missy asks, "Is that the Big Dipper?," pointing to a group of stars.

"I'm not great with constellations," Zach says softly, not taking his eyes off Missy.

Missy smiles and wonders if Zach can see her blushing before giving him a shove, tossing him into the lake.

Zach coughs up water he inhaled and stands up, splashing Missy.

Missy returns to the top of the dock for a running start and does a cannonball, joining Zach in water. The lake water is still cold, and Missy comes up shivering. Zach paddles over to her and she welcomes him with a playful splash before swimming away, taunting him to catch her. Seeing her devilish grin, Zach can't resist.

"I'm coming for you," he shouts as he swims after her.

Missy shrieks, paddling away as fast as she can, but Zach is a faster swimmer and quickly catches her. He wraps his arms around her waist and rocks her back and forth like he's going to toss her.

She wraps her arms tight around his neck. "You wouldn't dare," she says.

Zach enjoys holding her too much to drop her back in the water. Each time she thinks he's going to throw her, she tosses her head back, letting out a loud, throaty laugh. He thinks her laugh is the best sound he's ever heard.

Setting her down, he strokes her hair as his hand slides down her back, finding its way into hers. Floating side by side in the quiet, Missy points out a shooting star.

"You're shivering," Zach says, pulling Missy back into his arms.

He gently strokes Missy's cheek, smiling at the way the reflection of the moonlight makes her eyes twinkle. She rests her head on his chest with his arms wrapped tight around her.

He tilts her chin up toward him and leans down, putting his lips on hers. Her mouth gently meets his.

"Should we go find a slice of that pie?" Missy whispers, minutes later.

Walking hand in hand from the dock across the back lawn, Zach listens to the song of the cicadas and watches the fireflies blinking, reminding him of the slower rhythm of summer at the lake. He watches the moths dance in the porch light, wishing he were as free from worry.

He pulls Missy in again, kissing her softly.

"I want to show you somewhere special. Are you free tomorrow?" he asks.

"I'd like that," Missy agrees.

⌘

Arriving back at his father's house, Zach sits on the edge of the bed and kicks off his shoes. *Why did I tell her all that? She must think I'm a fool.*

However, there was something different about her that he was drawn to. She was the most genuine and authentic person he had ever met. This was quite refreshing, in stark contrast to his recent experience.

He's leaning back on his pillows and staring up at the ceiling when he feels his phone buzz. Tracey's name comes up on the caller ID.

"Where have you been? I've been calling you all day," Tracey nags.

"I was busy working," Zach says, noting the frustration in Tracey's voice.

"I was just thinking about you. I miss you."

"It's been a long day."

"I heard the news about the judge. What an idiot. Where are you, anyway?" she asks.

"I needed to get away and think."

"Don't take too long—we have tickets for the Children's Hospital Gala this weekend, and then I thought we would spend all day Sunday in bed."

"I'm in Pine Lake," he says, dragging his hand down his face in extreme irritation.

"Why would you be there?"

"I don't think you get it. Your dad left me in a huge mess."

There is a long pause.

"Tracey?"

"Listen, Daddy isn't responsible for any of these ridiculous charges. It's all just gotten out of hand. You'll see—give it a month, and you'll have your life back exactly like it was before."

"Seriously? Do you understand I'm facing felony charges and a five-million-dollar fine? My assets are frozen, and I could get

50

potentially thirty years in jail, while he's in hiding? How could he leave me here to take all the heat?"

He feels a surge of adrenaline and springs upright in bed.

"It's just been so stressful for him," Tracey says. "He needs time to get away and think, too. Frankly, I resent your tone after everything my family has done for you."

"Oh, I'm sorry, princess—I didn't realize I was supposed to be grateful for this situation."

"Exactly what are you insinuating?"

"I've worked with your dad long enough to know he doesn't do things on a whim. He carefully plans every detail. He knew."

"Stop it. He's not like that!"

"You have no idea who your dad is or what he's capable of."

Tracey's voice suddenly switches octaves to an unnerving coo.

"I think you need some time to cool down. We'll talk at the Gala on Saturday."

Zach rubs his forehead. Her voice grates on him, and he feels a headache coming on.

"Tracey, I am not coming home for a while. I need some space," Zach says. "I have to go."

He can still hear her high-pitched protests as he ends the call.

Exhausted from weeks of sleep deprivation amid nightmares concerning his shattered life, he closes the curtains and pulls off his jeans, tossing them on the floor.

Remembering the little drawing Emma made him, he picks up his pants and carefully pulls out the picture. Smiling, he props it against the desk lamp before climbing into bed, hoping for better dreams to come.

He decides to focus on the stick figure portrait of himself holding Emma and Missy's stick figure's hands under a rainbow in front of the lake, until he drifts out of consciousness.

Chapter 5

The crystal stemware sits drying on the lint-free dish towel as Catherine polishes the silver, making sure to get in all the nooks and crannies with the toothpicks, as her mom instructed her. She momentarily considers telling her mom that they won't need the crystal stemware and polished silver for a backyard barbecue with Blake, but thinks better of it, knowing her mom's feelings will be hurt. She'll start saying things like "Why do I even bother trying to make things nice if no one even cares," and then the crying and the pouting will start. The last thing she wants is a bunch of drama before her parents, Betsy and Harold Davis, meet her boyfriend.

Boyfriend? she seethes to herself. What an awkward term to use after the age of forty. She longs for something unwavering, dignified. *Fiancé,* and then *husband.*

Catherine decides to keep her thoughts to herself. She leans toward the open window, trying to breathe in some fresh air over the smell of the silver polish.

Betsy pulls out the fresh-picked crab meat and lemons from the refrigerator, ready to make her famous crab puffs.

"Mom, we don't need any more food; you've already made more than enough for everyone," Catherine says.

Betsy waves her off, grabbing the rest of the ingredients from the pantry before getting distracted. She's noticed the dining-room table-cloth is uneven. She adjusts it and stands back to admire her work.

"Kitty Cat, do you know where those crystal candlesticks are? The ones I gave you as a housewarming gift?"

"I'm not sure. That was, like, two lifetimes ago. The table looks fine as it is. Can you stop fussing over it now?" Catherine pleads.

"I think it needs a bit more dressing up, don't you?"

I just said it was fine, Catherine thinks, rolling her eyes and continuing to polish the silver.

"What are you doing, Mom?" Catherine asks, as she hears every door in the china cabinet swing manically open and shut.

"Like I said, I'm looking for the crystal candlesticks I gave you. They match the crystal salad bowl I thought we could use. I just know they'll turn up. Come help me find them."

Catherine puts down the silver breadbasket she was working on, removes her rubber gloves, and rubs her temples in frustration.

"Mom, I don't know where they are," she says through gritted teeth.

Betsy comes in and gives her a light swat on the bottom. "Tick-tock. Let's get going and find them."

"Actually, now that I think about it, I remember giving them to the charity drive last year."

"What? Why would you do that? Do you know how expensive those were?" Betsy shrieks.

"They weren't really my style, and I was decluttering," Catherine replies.

"I suppose *this* is your style," her mom says, picking up one of the Mason jars Catherine had placed on the table. The teal candle she'd put inside fell out and rolled to the corner of the room.

Catherine takes the Mason jar from her mom and collects the candle. "It's fresh rain scent. Aleksandra's favorite." Catherine smiles and puts it back in the center of the dining table.

"Rain? Harold, do you hear this? She expects me to serve beef wellington with a rain-scented candle burning on the table. Dinner is just ruined," Betsy cries.

"Mom, I told you Blake was going to grill some steaks and corn and we could eat out on the deck."

"Is that how you treat your guests, asking them to cook the dinner they were invited to? Well, it's no wonder."

"No wonder what? What's that supposed to mean? He's hardly a guest. I mean, we are practically engaged," she says.

"How would I know? You wouldn't even introduce us until now."

Catherine just bites her nails, not wanting to get into it with her mom, having to explain that *this* is exactly why she hadn't introduced Blake to them during the past two years.

"Stop chewing your nails—you know that's a vulgar habit," her mom says, grabbing her left hand and holding it up for inspection.

Her dad steps inside from the deck and puts his arm around Catherine's shoulder.

"Pumpkin, everything looks great," Harold says, kissing the top of Catherine's head.

She softens and wraps an arm around him. This sudden rise in temperature has become all too familiar, and her father knows just how to bring her back.

Harold walks over to Betsy, taking her hands. "Doll, you always make everything perfect. You know it will all turn out fine," he says, planting a kiss on her cheek.

"Oh, Harold, shoo. Let me go make those crab puffs," Betsy says, blushing at her husband's compliment.

Harold winks at Catherine and heads back out onto the deck.

Catherine hears the doorbell ring. *Thank God*, she thinks. "I'll get it," she calls out, racing to open the front door. She falls into Blake's arms, squeezing him tight.

"I'm so sorry for everything I said to you yesterday and everything I've ever done wrong. Please, please, please save me," Catherine pleads, looking into Blake's eyes.

"I'm glad to see you, too. Is it that bad?" Blake asks, rubbing her back and hugging her tight.

"You have no idea. I think we're on mimosa number six and she has achieved an advanced level of nagging. I feel like I'm twelve years old all over again."

"Breathe, honey. I'm here now and it's going to be great," Blake says optimistically.

"I'm not so sure about that," Catherine whispers as she leads Blake into the kitchen.

"Mom, this is Blake. Blake, this is my mom, Virginia."

"Oh, please, everyone calls me Betsy," she says, taking a break from stirring something on the stove. She adjusts her apron and pulls Blake in for a hug.

"Aren't you a looker. Catherine, why you didn't tell me he was so handsome?" Betsy asks, giving him a little pinch.

"I have, Mom, but thanks for making this weird."

"Okay, now, scoot. Take Blake out to relax on the deck while I finish up here," Betsy says.

Catherine nudges Blake toward the deck, where her father is working on the porch swing.

"Hey, Dad, can you come out from under there? Blake's here."

"What are you up to, sir?"

"I was just tightening the bolts. I have to make sure my little pumpkin is safe."

"Dad, I'm not a little girl anymore, and Blake just hung that a few months ago."

"Here, let me help you," Blake says, taking the wrench and crawling under the swing to tighten the bolts on the rear side.

Standing up, he presses down gently on the swing to test its sturdiness.

"See, pumpkin, Blake gets me. I'm Harold," her dad says.

"I leave you all alone for a minute and you're out here getting dirty," says Betsy, joining them. "Go wash up. I have cocktails and hors d'oeuvres," She says, in an upbeat singsong voice, twirling around with her silver platter before carefully setting it down on the patio table.

The men oblige, washing up in the kitchen, and soon they're all sitting down with their cocktails and crab puffs, enjoying the afternoon breeze and watching hummingbirds float around the feeders hanging on the deck.

"Mmm, mmm!" says Blake. "Betsy, these are amazing. Honey, did you show your parents the photos you took for the spring festival at the Nature Center? You won't believe the shots she captured. She took one of a black and blue butterfly on an orange milkweed plant that was amazing. She also caught a blue dragonfly on the dock."

"Don't forget the hummingbird I managed to snap taking a drink from the feeder," Catherine adds.

"That sounds great, pumpkin," Harold says.

"She has an amazing eye," Blake brags, wrapping his arm around her shoulder and giving her a gentle squeeze. "The sunset photo in the living room is one she took a few months back, and I had framed. I keep telling her she should sell them."

Catherine blushes at Blakes praise, "It's nice to have time for something I love."

"You're lucky he puts up with you and all of this," Betsy says, collecting their dishes.

Catherine cringes at her mom's words. Her mother always thought she had been a handful and made sure to remind Catherine every chance she could. Now, Catherine heard her mother's criticisms like a tape playing in her head. When she was a child it was because she was too energetic; *sit still.* In high school it was because she had too many hobbies; *what are you up to now.* As an adult it was her focus on work and Aleksandra. *I guess we are back to my hobbies.*

In the kitchen, Betsy rinses the dishes and then sets the dining-room table for dinner. She directs Harold to place the beef wellington in the center and she adds the bowls of potato salad and green salad to either side.

Once seated, Blake returns to the topic of Catherine's photography.

"Catherine also has a few of her prints hanging at the Pine View Inn. I'll show them to you when we go to the picnic this weekend," Blake says as they begin to eat.

Catherine smiles and looks at him, mouthing *Thank you.*

"And you're going to love Blake's renovation of the Pine View Inn. I don't know how he manages to modernize it while keeping all of its historic charm."

"It's not done yet, but it's coming along," Blake clarifies.

"Oh, darling, did you hear Lizzie just won the volunteer award at the club?"

Catherine feels her cheeks redden. She stabs some potato salad and shoves it in her mouth.

Catherine hears her mom calling her name and realizes she's tuned out during her mom's latest Lizzie update. She probably didn't miss much, as it's always the same. Her sister Lizzie is two years younger than her, and in her mom's eyes, she does everything right—the perfect daughter. She graduated from a prestigious college with honors, married a handsome and successful husband, does volunteer work, and dotes on her two perfect children. Makes Catherine want to gag.

Her mom always describes Catherine as her "difficult" child. She always took more risks than her sister, choosing to blaze her own trail, being a single mom to Aleksandra while building her career instead of finding a suitable husband. The move to Pine Lake and falling in love with Blake was just her latest escapade, in her mom's eyes. *How does she forget that I built a multimillion-dollar firm while raising Aleksandra on my own? Apparently, none of that matters if you don't have the right man by your side*, Catherine thinks, with an audible groan. She looks up and realizes everyone at the table is staring at her.

"Sorry, I got distracted," she apologizes.

"Dear, we are very worried about you," her mom begins.

"Mom, let's not do this again," Catherine says, rolling her eyes.

"I know things were hard after losing Aleksandra, and we were so patient, but it has been years now, and we think it's time to come back home and get back to your life."

"*Mom*," Catherine says, through gritted teeth.

"Did I hear Catherine mention your son is in town?" Harold asks, trying to change the subject.

"Yes, he has some business in town," Blake says.

"Business in town? How old is he?" Betsy asks.

"Thirty-two," Blake answers.

Betsy's mouth opens as if to speak, but nothing comes out.

"Can you pass the potato salad, please, Betsy?" Blake asks.

She nods and picks up the bowl, but drops it on the floor as she tries to pass it. "Thirty-two?" she questions.

"I was eighteen," Blake says, answering the question she didn't ask, bending down to pick up the pieces of the bowl and uses his napkin to clean up the spilled salad.

"Well, hopefully you'll make an honest woman out of this one," she prods, looking in Catherine's direction.

"Mom!" Catherine shrieks, embarrassed.

After dinner, Betsy insists on washing the dishes. She and Harold head into the kitchen and Catherine and Blake take their drinks out onto the deck to watch the sunset from the swing. Catherine rests her head on Blake's shoulder and closes her eyes, enjoying the rhythm of the swing.

"Was my mom flirting with you back there?" Catherine jokes.

"Not by the end, she wasn't. I'm surprised she didn't throw that potato salad at me. What's her deal with marriage, anyway?"

Catherine pushes her foot against the deck floor, to get the swing moving while she considers his question. She knows her mom didn't approve of her being a single mom and wants her to get married and settle down. Catherine wants that too, but she knows Blake's first marriage with Ginger has left him wary and she doesn't want to add any more pressure.

"I couldn't say. What's *your* deal with marriage?" Catherine asks, giving him a playful tickle.

"I just don't want a bunch of crazy talk to wreck a good thing."

"I don't know. Maybe she has a point."

"Don't let anyone try to rush things. We're happy here."

"Are we?" Catherine asks, lifting her head to look at him.

"I can't believe you would even ask me that." Blake shakes his head in disbelief.

"I mean, what's the problem? Why not me? We've been together all this time and...."

"Cat, we've been through this a hundred times. You know how things ended with Zach's mom, and how horrible my marriage with Ginger was. I just don't want to get married again."

Shortly after Catherine and Blake started dating she met Ginger and she they were nothing alike. After being together for two years she doesn't understand how Blake could think their relationship would be anything like his marriage with Ginger.

"But I'm not them. I just want us to be together forever."

60

"We don't have to be married to spend our future together."

"I know, but it's important to me," Catherine says.

"I'm a hundred percent with you, married or not. Isn't that enough?"

"I want more."

"So, what—if I won't marry you, then it's over?"

"I don't know," Catherine says.

She doesn't want to show too much emotion, yet she doesn't want him to leave.

Blake stands up from the swing. "I have to go," Blake says. "I want to cool off. You have fun with your parents."

From the back deck, Catherine hears the smack of the screen door as he storms out, quickly followed by the growl of his exhaust as his truck pulls out of the driveway.

She pushes herself on the swing, wondering why they can't have a productive conversation about their relationship. She replays his words in her mind, *I'm one hundred percent with you. Then why* does it always end with him rushing off and her feeling like she can't share how she truly feels about things? She wants to trust that he wants to be with her, but in moments like this, it's hard.

⚬

As night falls Missy takes one final walk through the Inn before heading down the long hallway from the main part of the Inn to their private apartment. She sinks into the soft comfort of her bed, taking a deep breath and exhaling the weight of her day. Rolling onto her side, she makes a mental list of everything she has yet to do before the tourist season starts. It feels like it's a mile long. With less than a week to go, she knows how busy her day will be tomorrow.

She wills sleep to come, and soon her eyes are heavy. Just as she starts to drift off, she hears Emma wailing from the next room.

She bolts upright, grabs her bathrobe, and hurries to Emma's room.

Throwing open Emma's door, she heads toward the bed and stubs her toe on the nightstand.

"Ouch," she says, falling onto the edge of the bed.

She pulls Emma into her arms. "Shhhh, it's okay," she whispers, rocking her gently. She can still feel the dampness of her hair from her evening bath and smell the lingering scent of her lavender shampoo.

"I heard a monster outside of my window," Emma sniffles.

"No, baby, it's probably just the wind blowing a tree branch," Missy reassures her. "Let's get some water, and then it's right back to bed."

Missy carries her daughter into the kitchen, setting her down on the island. She walks over to the window, peeling back the blinds just enough to peer out. She sees some light on the back lawn but can't see anyone out there. Rummaging through the kitchen drawers, she finds a flashlight and flips the switch on and off, making sure it works.

"Sit still until I come back," she instructs Emma.

Tiptoeing onto the back deck, she slowly shines the flashlight around, scanning the lawn.

"Who's out here?" Missy calls, her voice trembling.

When she reaches the edge of the deck, she can see Blake hunched over a table, comprised of a sheet of plywood over a couple of saw-horses. By the light of a battery-powered lantern, he's writing notes on what must be his construction plans, glancing at the stack of lumber and then back to the plans. His toolbox sits open nearby, and a power drill and table saw are set up on the plywood table. She watches as he carefully measures a board, makes marks with a pencil, then tucks it behind his ear. Then he repeats the measuring and marking again before running the board through the saw.

Emma squeals and covers her ears. "The monster!"

"Didn't I say to sit still? What are you doing out here?" Missy says, scooping Emma up into a hug to comfort her. When the sound of the saw stops, Blake blows the sawdust off his board and stands back, admiring his handiwork.

Missy coughs, "Ahem."

Blake turns and sees Missy in her bathrobe, tapping her foot and bouncing Emma on her hip. Before she can tuck her head into Missy's shoulder, Blake sees that Emma has been crying.

"I don't mean to interrupt your rhythm, but it's late, and Emma needs her sleep." Missy calls out.

Blake puts the board down and brushes off his hands as he walks over.

"I'm sorry, kiddo—did I scare you?" Blake asks, tousling Emma's hair. "I didn't even realize it had gotten so dark."

"Blake, it's ten o'clock!" Missy laughs and then turns to her daughter. "You can see there isn't anything scary, just Mr. Blake and his tools, so scoot on back to bed." Missy puts Emma down and gives her bottom a little pat. The night is chilly, and Emma runs back inside.

"I really am sorry. I didn't even think of the noise and how late it was. I was worried about staying on schedule. Since you're here now, can I show you what I'm working on?" Blake asks cautiously.

"I know you won't stop till I give in, so go ahead."

"You mentioned you wanted the gazebo close to the water, but I thought it would fit better over here in the garden," Blake says.

Missy looks towards the water and then at Blake's new location before nodding her head in agreement. "I think that will work. Having some events here could really save our hide. Plus, I know just who the first wedding reservation could be," she says with a wink.

Blake avoids her glance, walking past her to collect his things. "I have enough to deal with right now without a wedding on my plate."

Missy crosses her arms and glares at Blake. "Out with it. Tell me what you're really doing back here this late?"

Blake sets his tools down and leans against the sawhorse table.

"Catherine's mom is pushing this idea of a wedding," Blake begins.

"Well, you two *are* perfect together."

"There was something in Catherine's eyes when her mom was talking about it," Blake says.

"What woman wouldn't be excited at the idea of marrying the man she loves?"

"Or maybe like every other woman, she just thinks a man only loves her if she's wearing a big fat fancy ring."

Missy shakes her head. "You know she isn't like that. Have you talked to her about this?"

"Why does she have to go changing something good? Marriage ruins everything. You know how after I married Ginger, it just turned into nagging and bitterness and complaining. I don't want that to happen with Catherine."

"Until his last days, Granddaddy called Ya-Ya his sunshine, and they were married for more than sixty years."

"I think they were the exception to the rule." Blake shrugs and looks around at the mess he's made.

"You know I can't stay mad at you, but maybe next time you can just talk to Catherine instead of making a racket on my lawn," Missy says.

"Got it, boss," Blake teases, loading the truck to head out.

Missy heads back in. She closes the kitchen curtains and makes sure all the lights are off before checking on Emma. She adjusts her blankets, pulling them up over her shoulders and kissing her head.

"Good night, baby girl," she whispers, and heads back to bed.

Chapter 6

Early the next morning Zach pulls up to the Inn and heads down to boat docks. The Inn has a motorboat to take guests out on the lake for tours and water sports and Missy agreed to let him use it for a surprised he planned for Missy and Emma. He pulls back the nylon cover and folds it. Just as he stows it away, he sees Emma barreling across the back lawn to the dock with Missy trailing behind. Taking Emma by the hand, he walks over to Missy to grab her beach bag overflowing with the beach towels, sunscreen, a picnic basket, and a thermos of cold water. Securing Emma's life vest, he hoists her into the back of the boat and lends Missy a hand as she steps on board. Smiling at Missy, Zach gives the boat some gas and watches as Missy's hair blows in the breeze, nearly taking her hat with it.

They motor about ten miles south down the lake to White Oak Cove, where they slow down to a crawl. White Oak Cove is a nature preserve, which means there are no houses dotting the shoreline. Water sports are prohibited, so very few boats come down this far into the lake. The edge of the lake is lined with cattails and tall grasses, creating a small marsh surrounded by a dense grove of white oak and mixed pine trees. As they float deeper into the cove, Zach points to a blue heron perched on a fallen oak tree, its eyes scanning the lake for small fish to eat. When it finds one, it lifts off and its dagger-like beak dips below the surface before it flies back to the fallen tree.

At the end of the cove, Zach sets the anchor and Missy blows up Emma's pirate ship floatie and ties it to the back of the boat before Emma jumps off the stern to play. Missy and Zach relax on the boat's cushioned sun lounger, watching as Emma plays in the lake, asking them to watch her do tricks and jump off her floatie.

"I can't remember the last time I had such a relaxing afternoon," Zach says.

"I know what you mean. Between Emma and the Inn, I hardly ever get any time off," Missy says.

"What's your idea of a perfect day?" Zach asks.

Missy leans back on the sun lounger, closing her eyes for a second and feeling the sun on her face as she thinks about Zach's question. Propping herself up on her elbows, she replies, "This. I think this is pretty much my perfect day. Relaxing on the water with someone that sparks something in my heart while Emma plays nearby. I don't think it gets much better than this."

Zach thinks about the large house he bought a few years ago on Lake Harriet. He hoped that he would share it with a wife and kids, but the halls echo from emptiness rather than ring with sounds of love and laughter. He wanted to know the frustration of setting an important file down on the kitchen counter only to pick it up and find it sticky from a discarded peanut butter and jelly sandwich, or the annoyance of cleaning the dogs' messy footprints off the foyer floors for the tenth time in one day during the muddy spring season.

He wanted to know what it felt like to fight for someone you love in moments when you wonder why you love them, but then fall onto the couch as darkness falls and feel her head on your shoulder and smell the familiar scent of her shampoo. He wanted to do life with someone at his side who knows all of his flaws and doesn't want to be anywhere else but with him.

"I think you're right," he agrees simply, without sharing how much he has gotten it wrong.

She reaches across the sun lounger, her fingers sliding between his with ease. He smiles, then wonders what she would think if she knew everything about him.

When they are all tired of taking jumps off the boat and swimming around the cove, they anchor the boat at a nearby beach to enjoy their picnic. After scarfing down a sandwich, Emma runs off to build sandcastles near the water's edge. Missy and Zach relax on their blanket, talking and enjoying the picnic lunch Missy packed. When Emma begins to get fussy from their long day in the sun, they pack up the picnic and floaties and motor back to the Inn. On the way, Emma falls asleep on the back seat, curled up under her towel.

Zach helps Missy and Emma off the boat and Emma races across the lawn and into the Inn. Missy watches her, amazed at how a quick nap can reenergize her. Pausing at the deck, Missy thanks Zach for the fun day, and invites him to join her and her girlfriends that evening at Nate's Bar, for an open mic night.

He agrees, and they part with a kiss.

Back at Blake's, Zach finishes getting ready. He rolls up the sleeves of his shirt and runs a comb through his hair, checking his reflection. He grabs his jacket and, remembering his cards don't work, grabs the envelope from his bedside table. He pockets all the cash and carelessly tosses the empty envelope onto his bed before racing downstairs. His phone rings on the way.

"Scott, how's it going?" Zach says, answering his phone.

"Hey, you got a second?" Scott asks.

"Can it wait? I am actually headed out."

"You're supposed to be clearing your head so you can focus on your trial, not goofing off," Scott says.

"I haven't forgotten about my situation."

"Look, I was talking to the prosecutor and they've made an offer,"

"Break it down for me. What's the worst-case scenario?"

"Well, you're still looking at a five-million-dollar fine, but they've dropped it to just ten years in jail."

Zach falls against the door behind him.

"No way—that's not good enough. You have to get them to do better."

"I'm doing my best, Zach."

"Well, tell them I'm not interested in their offer. I'm not going to pay a fine and spend a decade in prison for something I didn't do."

He ends the call before Scott can say anything else.

"Damn it!" he shouts, throwing his phone into the mudroom.

He runs his hands through his hair and sighs heavily. In the mudroom he sees a laundry basket lying on its side with socks and shirts tumbling out, all over the floor. Looking up, he sees Catherine trying to hide behind the door.

All the color drains from his face.

"I didn't know anyone was home," Zach says.

"I just came back for my charging cord—and then I knocked over the basket, trying to give you some privacy," Catherine says.

Zach bends down, picking up the clean laundry and placing it back into the basket.

"I guess you heard all that?" Zach asks, looking her in the eye.

"Well, you were on speakerphone. Ten years' jail time and five million dollars doesn't sound good," she replies.

"It's not what you think," Zach responds, slumping to the ground.

Catherine nods.

"That deal I told you about didn't go well. I am being charged with securities fraud. My lawyer wants me to turn in my associates in exchange for the deal. Like a plea bargain."

"But you don't want to?"

Zach shakes his head. "Scott said it's a good deal. If I turn in Mr. Anderson, I get twenty years shaved on my sentence, but I still have the five million dollar fine. I guess I just don't feel I deserve the fine, or the jail time."

"I have done forensic accounting for other cases, maybe I could take a look at things," Catherine offers.

"It's ok, I don't want to drag you into my mess,"

"Is that why you came here? To hide from all this?" she asks.

"Not exactly. My lawyer, he's a friend of mine. He all but shoved me on the plane, telling me I need to take some time to clear my head."

"But you haven't told your father?"

Zach avoids her eyes, scooping the clothes into the basket.

"Answer me—does he know about any of this?"

Standing up, Zach sets the laundry basket on the dryer and shakes his head. "Just promise you won't tell my dad what you heard."

"Do you understand what you're asking me to do? I can't lie to your dad."

"He won't understand. I just need some more time to figure this all out, okay?" And with that, Zach brushes past her on his way out the door.

Catherine carries the laundry basket with her as she heads upstairs for her phone cord. As she passes Zach's door, she looks around before setting the basket down and turning the doorknob. *Just going to take a peek*, she tells herself.

Inside she sees his room is neat as a pin and bed is perfectly made. *This is fine; I'm just concerned and trying to help*, she tells herself.

She finds an envelope on the bed and can't contain her curiosity. Opening it, she finds it empty, but can't stop searching.

Rifling through the drawer in the bedside table, she discovers an airline boarding pass with a 6:45 p.m. departure. With the flight time and drive from the city, he had to have come straight here. *There never was a meeting in the city*, she realizes, then chastises herself. *What are you doing, spying on him?* She puts the boarding pass back in the drawer.

⁂

Shaking off his encounter with Catherine, Zach hops into his rental car and throws it in reverse without even checking the mirror. He drives through town looking for Nate's Bar. When he pulls up to the tavern, he notices the white banner advertising the open mic night Missy had mentioned. Off the beaten path, the tavern isn't the type of place tourists usually visit.

He opens the door and is greeted with the smell of stale beer and cigarettes, even though smoking indoors has been banned for years. Once his eyes adjust to the dim light, he looks around for Missy but doesn't see her. He finds a seat at the end of the bar, as far away as he can get from the makeshift stage which holds a microphone and bar stool, and texts her that he's there.

"What'll you have?" the bartender asks.

"Do you have a Moon and Stars IPA?"

"One Yuengling, coming right up." The bartender tilts the glass under the tap and fills it with cold amber beer.

Zach stares into his beer, sipping slowly, replaying his conversation with Scott.

How could he spend the next ten years of his life in jail? Or if he refused the plea deal, he could spend even more time there. But how could he help the federal government build a case to put Mr. Anderson away for the rest of his life?

He considered his options, but drew a blank. *Either way I will have a felony record and have to pay five million dollars. The government is making an example out of me and trying to scare me into telling them what they want to know.*

Zach drains his beer and slams the mug on the bar. He hears a group of girls laughing loudly as they enter the bar. He spots Missy among them and immediately scans the area for a way to leave, unnoticed. Finding none, he just looks down at the bar, trying to be invisible.

"I think this night calls for something stronger than beer," Missy says, sneaking up behind him.

He turns around at the sound of her voice, eyeing her tan legs shown to full advantage in her denim mini skirt. Her eyes sparkle beneath a hint of eye shadow.

She climbs onto the empty barstool next to him.

"He'll have a double," she says, holding Zach's glass up to the bartender. "My girlfriend thinks she's the next Janis Joplin, and she's here for her big break," she laughs, pointing over to where her friends have settled at a table. "Let's go," she says, grabbing his hand and leading the way over to her friends.

"Ladies, this is Zach. Zach, meet the girls."

"Let's get a round for the table," one of the women cheers.

The server soon brings drinks and appetizers for the table.

"Woohoo!" one of Missy's friends yelps as they all clink glasses and take a drink.

"Looks like you girls came to party," Zach shouts over the noise of the bar.

"Just six single women living the dream." Missy laughs and cheers as another singer finishes a song and the DJ announces a break and turns on a slow song.

"Dance with me?" Missy asks.

"I'm not much of a dancer," Zach says.

"Just one," Missy says. She takes him by the hand and leads him onto the dance floor.

Zach puts his arm around her waist and takes her hand in his. Missy leans in and rests her head on his shoulder and breathes in the musky scent of his cologne. *Why do men smell so good?* she thinks. Zach moves his hand around her waist, holding her close and breathing in the lavender scent of her hair.

"She's up next!" Missy's friend yells loudly from the table.

"I guess we should go back," Missy says, not moving from Zach's embrace. She wraps her fingers around his and smiles as they return to the table.

Her friend nervously approaches the microphone and drops it as she attempts to release it from the stand. She smiles sheepishly at the hollering table of friends before her music starts.

"Prove that you love me and buy the next round..." As she croons the line from the Janis Joplin song, everyone in the bar gets to their feet and erupts into cheers. By the time the song finishes, the applause is thunderous.

Missy and her friends rush to hug and congratulate her, but the celebration is short-lived, as the next singer has already started a fast-paced country song, and the girls have pushed their chairs aside to start a choreographed line dance. The men at the next table stand up to join them. Everybody seems to know what they're doing except Zach.

"Come on," Missy calls to Zach, waving him over.

"I'm good," he answers, sitting down at the table, happy to watch.

One of the men sidles up to Missy, wraps his arms around her waist, and leans in to whisper something. Missy laughs and gracefully spins away, putting some distance between them. The man misses a step, bumping into Missy and pouring his beer down her back. Missy shrieks and shoves the guy, but he continues laughing and tries to grab her again.

"Wet T-shirt contest!" he shouts, encircling her from behind.

Zach sees Missy trying to squirm free, but the drunk guy doesn't seem to notice, and is trying to plant a kiss on her neck.

Zach jumps up from his seat and heads over.

"Hey, buddy, maybe you want to sit this one out," Zach begins, grabbing him by the shoulder.

"No, sir," the man says, eyeing Missy and licking his lips.

Zach pulls the guy back, trying to release Missy from his grasp, but he doesn't gain an inch.

"Get your hands off her," Zach shouts.

The bar goes quiet and the guy still doesn't let go of Missy.

"I can handle it, Zach," Missy says, trying to squirm away.

"You her old man?" the guy sputters.

"Just take a hint—she's not interested," Zach retorts.

The guy turns his back on Zach and continues to grope Missy, moving his hands down her body.

Zach grabs the guy's arm and spins him around so they're face-to-face.

"Why don't you and your fancy suit go back to where you came from?" the man says.

Zach takes a swing and lands his fist on the guy's cheekbone.

The girls scream and Missy tugs at Zach. But he brushes her off, staring down his opponent.

"Zach, stop!" Missy says, grasping his sleeve.

The drunk guy is a sweaty mess. He reeks of beer, and spits on Zach's face, right before landing a punch on Zach's jaw.

Zach can hear nothing but the blood thumping in his ears. He thinks of how Mr. Anderson bullied him and took advantage of so many people just to get what he wanted. As he throws a punch, he thinks, *You can't just take whatever you want whenever you want. I won't let you.* He has no idea how many punches he lands on the guy before the bouncers pull him off.

He wipes the spit off his face and shouts, "She's too good for you. Keep your hands off of her."

The bouncers drag him outside, and he keeps his head down as they pass Missy. He can't bear to see the look of fear and hurt in her eyes.

"I'll take it from here."

Zach glances toward the familiar voice and sees his cousin Tim, who's been in the local police force for years. Tim carefully guides Zach into the back of the police vehicle, protecting his head as he slides into the backseat.

Starting the car, Tim says, "I heard you were back in town. Guess I was hoping to catch up under different circumstances."

There are less than twelve hundred residents in Pine Lake and I have to be arrested by one I'm related to Zach thinks as he stares out the window, trying to ignore the throbbing pain in his jaw. Licking his lips, he tastes blood.

"Man, I didn't expect to pick you up. I heard you've been doing real well for yourself these days," Tim says.

"Something like that," Zach answers, still looking out the window.

"How long has it been?" Tim continues, trying to lighten the mood. "We really had some good times back in the day, didn't we? Remember that night you, me, and Joey took the police car from the state park dock and went for a nighttime ride? Now look at me, wearing the uniform." Tim laughs, taking a bite of his gas station hot dog and dripping mustard onto his uniform pants. "Want a bite?" he asks, with his mouth full.

Zach waves off the offer.

A few minutes later they pull into the station. Tim opens the back door of the patrol car and helps Zach out. As they step into the station, Zach feels a chill go up his spine as he takes in the lobby.

The fluorescent lights shine a cool unwelcoming light onto the hard tile floor. The molded plastic chairs and the gray paint on the walls leave Zach feeling even more depressed.

Tim motions to one of the chairs in the lobby. "Just wait here. I'm not going to throw you in lockup."

Zach sits down and leans his head against the wall, closing his eyes.

Tim returns with an ice pack. "Sheriff already called your dad to pick you up."

"Great. Memory lane *and* a lecture," Zach says sarcastically.

Tim sits down next to Zach, resting his elbows on his knees. "Missy is like a sister to all of us around here, so don't mess with her. Understood?"

Zach nods silently and leans his head against the wall, once again closing his eyes. "I don't think we need to worry about that anymore."

"Look, I gotta get back to work, but don't be such a stranger round here," Tim says, and gives his knee a tap.

The woman at the desk slides open the bulletproof-glass panel and pushes a phone through. "Call for you," she says to Zach.

"It was good to see you, buddy," Tim says, standing to leave.

Zach nods and picks up the call.

"I thought we were past this nonsense," Blake shouts from the other end of the phone.

"Uh-huh," Zach answers, leaning back in his chair.

"Where did I go wrong?" Blake continues.

Zach adjusts his ice pack and asks, "Do you think you could pick me up and we could do the lecture tomorrow?"

"I tried to raise you better than this," Blake says.

"Ha. Raise me? What are you even talking about? Don't worry—there's no way you could've done anything wrong when you weren't even there!" Zach shouts.

"I think you need to stay there for the night and think about what you're doing with your life," Blake says.

"You know I'm a grown man, not a child?"

"Then start acting like one," Blake says.

Zach slams down the phone.

Looking up, Zach notices the woman behind the glass glaring at him and offers her an embarrassed wave as an apology for getting so animated. He passes the phone back to her and pauses to consider his options. No taxis or Ubers in Pine Lake, so he resigns himself to waiting for his dad or getting a ride from Tim when his shift ends.

He closes his eyes, trying to block out the blinking fluorescent lights and get comfortable in the molded plastic chair. Folding his arms across his chest he sighs. *It's going to be a long night.*

Chapter 7

*B*lake sets the phone down on the bed and feels Catherine roll over, her sleep interrupted by his shouting at Zach. He can't stop the rant going on in his head. *Zach thinks he knows everything, but really he is just immature, and careless, and stupid. He never asks for advice and that's why he makes so many mistakes. At his age I'd been working, running my business, and taking care of a family for years. Why can't he just get it together?*

Blake runs back his catalog of complaints about his son and double-checks his list. *Yup, immature was on it*, he thinks to himself. *Why doesn't Zach just ask for advice instead of getting himself into messes like this and then looking to me to fix it for him?*

Of course, Zach thinks I shouldn't have worked so many hours—that I should've just followed them across the country when Jenny moved to Minnesota, so I could've spent more time with him. That's part of Zach's problem. He lives in a fairy-tale world instead of understanding why that wouldn't have worked. Jenny and I agreed she should move across the country so they would have the support of her parents. How does Zach think the bills would have been paid if I was sitting on the floor playing trains with him? I made sure he always had food to eat and clothes to wear. His needs were taken care of. Why can't Zach accept that I did my best. Isn't it time for him grow up and stop blaming me?

Amid his pacing back and forth across the bedroom, Blake announces, "Zach has been picked up and is at the sheriff's station. Apparently he got into a fight at Nate's Bar."

Catherine jumps up from bed, fumbling around in the dark looking for her clothes.

"Hurry up and get dressed," she says, throwing him a shirt.

He catches it before it hits his face. "I'm not going," Blake responds sharply.

"What do you mean, you aren't going?"

"I think he needs to sleep it off overnight and learn his lesson."

"I'm sorry, what?" Catherine says, flipping on the bedside lamp and staring at Blake.

"This is what he does," Blake says, recounting how Zach would sneak out in the middle of the night as a teenager and toilet-paper another teen's home or drink a few beers down by the lake and get picked up by the police, and he would have to go rescue him and sort things out.

"I cannot believe you. That's how it works with kids, and he's not a teenager anymore! For years, I've listened to you go on and on about how you wish you had a relationship with Zach, and now that he truly needs you, you aren't going to be there for him?"

"Don't turn this around on me. I'm not doing anything wrong here," Blake says.

"Has it occurred to you that all Zach wants is for you to love him and show up for him when he needs you? Just be there for him."

"I never did anything as stupid as this. He's out of control."

"Yay, congratulations to you. You've never made a mistake in your life."

Blake just glares in response.

Catherine sits down on the bed and takes a deep breath. She takes Blake's hand. Lowering her voice, she tries reasoning with him.

"Maybe he came here because he needs your love and support. Maybe he needs your help right now."

"I can't believe you're taking his side," Blake says, taking his hand from Catherine's.

"I can't believe you're not!" Catherine says, standing up.

"He's my son and I know what is best for him," Blake says.

No, you don't. You're never there for him, and you're never there for me, Catherine thinks.

"If you go get him, don't bring him back here. In fact, don't come back here at all," Blake shouts.

Catherine throws her hair into a messy bun and races down the stairs. She grabs a sweater and her keys and slams the front door as she hurries out of the house to her car.

Speeding down the road toward the police station, she sees a deer leap into the road and stop on the center line. Slamming on her brakes, Catherine brings the car to a stop and waits for the deer to finish crossing. She feels her heart pounding and takes a deep breath before continuing. Driving more slowly and carefully down the dark curvy roads, scanning the edges for deer, she soon finds her mind replaying the scene with Blake.

Despite Blake wanting to be closer with Zach and wishing they had a better relationship, here he is, abandoning his son yet again. Why can't he be compassionate and give Zach the benefit of the doubt? Why does he jump straight to judging him and keeping score of every mistake he has ever made?

Catherine remembers being a parent—sleepless nights when Aleksandra snuck out to a party with her friends and then called, needing a ride; coming home in the middle of the night from a sleepover after having a fight with a friend. Catherine always felt it was part of her job as a parent to be a place of comfort and support. The world can be a harsh-enough critic without a parent being a source of judgment. That didn't mean she would just agree with Aleksandra or overlook her transgressions. Of course, there was a time and place for consequences, but first and foremost her job was to show love and kindness and to listen. Why doesn't Blake get it? Why can't he show up for Zach?

She sees the station lights up ahead. Slowing down, she pulls into the parking lot and takes a moment to shake off her frustration with Blake before heading in for Zach.

⧂

Zach shifts in his chair, trying to get comfortable, and checks his watch. He sighs, adjusting his ice pack, settling in for more hours of waiting. He hears the station door open but doesn't move. A chair screeches on the floor beside him, and he still doesn't move or open his eyes.

"Shall we do this now or later?" Zach asks.

"Do what?" Catherine asks.

Zach takes the ice pack off his face and looks at Catherine. "I thought you were my dad."

"Nope, it's just me," Catherine says.

"I assumed he was going to give me another lecture about how I should grow up and not behave so stupidly."

"It's late," Catherine says. "Let's get out of here."

Stepping outside, Zach takes in the stars in the night sky and feels his shoulders relax as he walks to the car. Taking in a deep breath of the cool night air, he opens the car door and slides in, feeling relieved Catherine isn't making a big deal out of this, showing up for him even though she barely knows him.

Catherine tries breaking the silence. "You know your dad loves you."

"He has an interesting way of showing it."

Zach stares out the window, lost in his thoughts. *How can his dad think it's okay to offer judgment on his life after he was absent for most of it? Where was he when he was learning to ride his first two-wheeler, or learning to drive, or heading off on his first date? Aren't dads supposed to teach you how to do those things? Isn't that their job? All his dad knows how to do is put a check in the mail and criticize his choices.*

"He's trying," Catherine offers.

"How can you defend him?"

Catherine struggles to answer honestly. She doesn't agree with how Blake is handling things with Zach, and she knows that Zach has every right to feel the way he does. It's not fair for her to minimize his feelings, so she stays silent.

Minutes later Catherine pulls the car into her driveway and turns toward Zach, wanting to tell him all the great things he doesn't see about Blake, but his expression looks as bruised as his face, so she just turns the car off and they head inside.

Catherine shows him to her guest room, asking if he'll be okay.

"Yeah. I think my ego is more bruised than my body," Zach says, trying to smile.

Catherine laughs. "Do you need anything?"

"I'm just going to bed," Zach says.

Catherine heads to her room for the night. She peels off her jeans and sweatshirt and crawls into bed. Exhausted, she soon drifts off to sleep.

The next morning, Catherine rolls over and reaches for Blake before remembering their fight and her drive back to her own home. She blinks her eyes open, squinting from the sunshine streaming through the windows.

She reaches to the nightstand and picks up her phone, looking for a text or missed call from Blake. Nothing. She throws on her jeans and sweatshirt from the night before and goes to the kitchen to make coffee. Before it has finished brewing, Zach joins her in the kitchen.

"You look awful," Catherine says.

Zach just nods and tries to comb his hair with his fingers and straighten out his rumpled shirt.

"There's coffee," Catherine says, giving him an empathetic smile.

"Thanks," Zach says, collapsing into the nearest chair.

Catherine brings him some water and Advil and Alka-Seltzer. "Take these. You'll feel better, I promise."

Zach rests his elbows on the table to hold his head up.

"I just wanted to apologize—"

"No need," Catherine says, putting her hand on Zach's. "We've all done our fair share of stupid things."

"Thanks," Zach says.

"I spent some time online yesterday," Catherine says. "You can learn a lot about people on the Internet."

"You can't believe everything you read," he groans. "Some sites need juicy gossip to get more views to please their advertisers."

"Do you believe the saying, where there's smoke, there's fire?"

"Touché," Zach says, leaning back in his chair, considering how much to share.

"So, is any of it true?" she asks.

"You're not going to let this go, are you?"

82

Catherine shakes her head before taking another sip of her coffee.

"You know, you're worse than the FBI," Zach says.

"Why, thank you."

"It wasn't a compliment."

Catherine makes them each a plate of scrambled eggs and bacon with toast and tops off their coffees.

Trying to figure out where to start, Zach stares up at the ceiling, as if the answers are printed up there. Picking at his food, he replays his past in his mind, and finally begins.

"I trusted some people I shouldn't have. I think I was blinded by the promise of big money."

"What do you mean?" Catherine asks.

"When I first met Bill Anderson, when I was a teenager, he seemed like good guy. He was successful, but he still made time for his family. Then maybe he changed, or maybe I changed. I don't know."

Catherine tilted her head, waiting for him to go on.

"I can still remember my first day at work like it was yesterday," Zach says. He tells her about starting his career with Anderson International, pulling into the visitor parking lot of the building and checking the time. He was early. He watched a stream of cars heading into the employee garage. Checking the time again, he adjusted his tie, grabbed his briefcase, and took one last look at his reflection before heading toward the main entrance.

The building was brand-new, a towering white structure with their logo perched on top in blue. It had a grand lobby: marble floors beneath a towering ceiling, with windows from floor to ceiling letting in the morning light. Checking in at Security to get his visitor badge, he watched the hustle and bustle of the employees, all in navy blue or black suits, rushing past him. Their workday had already started, and they were chattering among themselves and on their cell phones. Starbucks cups in hand, they were rushing for the elevators.

He felt the butterflies in his stomach, excited to be part of the corporate world.

He joined the employees headed to the elevators and pressed the button for the fifteenth floor. As he stepped off the elevator, a woman behind a tall mahogany desk with fresh flowers on the corner directed him to a visitors' area. The sofas and oversized chairs in the waiting room were more suited for a formal living room than traditional office decor. He was impressed. He had never been in an office like this, and he liked it. After a lifetime of coupon-clipping and thrift-store clothes, he was looking forward to being able to buy things he had only dreamed of as a kid.

But once he'd gotten started in the job, over time, it became about more than that. He still loved his custom suits and exotic cars, but he was addicted to the thrill and the challenge of closing bigger and bigger deals.

"I guess I got hungry for this huge deal, and it made me careless," Zach says, his chin quivering. He shoves his chair back and moves to refill his coffee, but just stands facing the coffeepot. He rests his palms on the counter, letting out a deep breath.

"I was suspicious, and it didn't take too much digging to realize the numbers didn't make sense. There was a sixty percent increase in revenue in the last fiscal year. The contracts were signed and executed but none of the invoices were paid. All three of the new contracts came from companies Mr. Anderson held shares in. Each time I tried to talk to him about it, he made me doubt myself. Then I'd end up apologizing for offending him. It was like he was a magician."

"Sounds more like a con artist to me," Catherine said.

"But Mr. Anderson was more than a just a boss and mentor. He was like a father to me. I trusted his word. I believed him," he says.

"What does your lawyer say?"

Zach turns around to face Catherine, leaning back against the counter and shoving his hands in his pockets.

"He wants you to share what you know, but that will implicate Mr. Anderson?" Catherine asks.

Zach nods.

Zach looks down at his feet before looking at Catherine. "I guess that's what I came here to figure out," he says.

"Pine Lake is a good place for that," she says. "Oh, shoot—I'm late for my meeting, and I still have to call the plumber," Catherine says, putting her coffee cup into the sink.

"I'm actually pretty handy," Zach says. "I can take a look at it and try to fix the problem before you get home," he suggests.

Catherine shows him what is wrong and then heads out.

Zach sits down and finishes his cup of coffee, thinking about what Catherine said.

He has always believed himself to be a man of action, making deals happen. He has never been the victim, at least he didn't think so, but maybe he is in this situation.

Chapter 8

Stepping up onto Catherine's front porch, Missy feels the midday sun on her bare shoulders. The winters are long in Pine Lake, and the warmth of the early summer sun on her skin feels refreshing. The front door is open, so she gently raps on the screen door and waits. When there's no answer, she knocks again and then tries the handle; finding it unlocked, she lets herself in.

Stepping into the foyer, Missy calls out, "Hello? Catherine, are you home?"

With no answer, she walks down the hallway and into the great room. Setting the pie she's brought with her down on the kitchen island, she digs around in her purse for a pen and paper to leave a note. Chewing on the pen cap, she looks out the back windows onto the lake, taking in the beautiful sunny day. She imagines relaxing on the deck, enjoying some girl talk with an iced tea and a slice of Ya-Ya's lemonade pie. Lately she's been feeling so overwhelmed, between taking care of Emma and Ya-Ya and the Inn, and then there's Zach. She doesn't have time for a distraction right now, but she can't help herself. He's handsome and smart, but even more than that, he is kind and gentle. Other than Granddaddy, she really hasn't met many men who are so open and easy to talk to. And he makes her laugh, and that's not easy to do. Catherine would understand.

"Hey, Missy," Zach says from behind her.

Startled, she jumps and throws her pen across the room.

"What are you doing here?" Missy asks.

Zach scratches his head, "My dad thought I should spend a night in the station to learn my lesson, but Catherine picked me up and let me stay the night. She had an issue with her sink, and I offered to fix it. A way to say thank you, I guess" Zach says, running the faucet and looking under the sink before wiping his hands off on a towel. "Good as new," he says.

"I wanted to drop off this lemonade pie that Ya-Ya made for Catherine," Missy says.

"I'm actually glad to see you," Zach says.

Missy blushes.

"I wanted to apologize for my behavior last night. I just got so angry watching that guy disrespect you," Zach says.

"I think I can handle myself," Missy says.

"I know you can," Zach says. And then adds, "You know you don't always have to be so strong."

Missy imagines music playing, like in a romantic film. The hunky lead would take this moment to scoop her into his arms, whispering something romantic, like "I will always protect you." Missy would melt into his arms and the hunky guy would lean in for a kiss. Of course, they would then live happily ever after without any stress or worries.

Missy laughs at her magical thinking and notices Zach is staring at her.

"Well, I'm just going to leave her a note and put the pie in the fridge," she says, embarrassed.

"Looks delicious," he says, reaching out a finger to swipe a taste.

Missy slaps his hand playfully. "Don't you dare!"

Zach grabs the pie from her. "Finders keepers!"

"What are you, five? This is for Catherine," she says, taking the pie back. "Will you tell her I stopped by? On second thought, I don't think this pie is safe here with you." She picks it up to take with her.

"I was thinking about going down to say hi to Catherine's horses. Join me?" he asks.

"I should probably get back." She steps toward the door, but Zach catches her hand, taking it into his, and she turns back.

"Do you have to?"

"We are so busy preparing for the Slice of Summer Picnic this weekend."

"You still do that?" Zach asks, suddenly flooded with memories of the festivities.

"Of course, it's tradition. Have you been?"

"Yeah, I used to visit my dad's family for Memorial Day each summer, and we would always go."

"So, you know it's a big deal for the whole town. This is our sixty-fifth summer opening."

"I know, but work will always be there, so why don't you join me for a horseback ride first," Zach teases.

Missy smiles and pretends to think about it for a second.

"Deal," she says, holding her hand out to shake on it.

Zach puts away his tools and cleans up around the sink, then leads them down to the barn where they tack up the horses and head for the wooded trail. Summer comes slowly to the mountains and as Memorial Day approaches, the trees are just starting to get green, and the sun peeks through the leaves, dancing like glitter in the streams full of melted snow and spring rains. The horses wander along the familiar path in the woods. In the quiet, Missy feels her shoulders relax from the stress and tension she didn't even realize she was holding so tightly. After meandering through the woods for a few miles, they reach a clearing that opens into a mature apple orchard. Each tree has a few white blossoms just opening from their branches. They tether the horses and find a clearing.

"It's beautiful back here. I didn't even know this trail existed," Missy says.

"This orchard belongs to my grandparents," Zach says. "My grand-dad taught me to ride when I was younger, and we would come out here to check on his trees."

Zach spreads out the blanket he brought and invites Missy to join him. Missy tries to imagine a young Zach riding through the orchard, helping his granddad, and smiles at the thought.

As if reading her mind, Zach starts to tell her more about his childhood.

"I didn't spend much time with my dad growing up. It was just short, sporadic visits. A Memorial Day weekend one summer and maybe a Fourth of July weekend the next," Zach begins. He goes on to tell her about some summers in high school that he spent in Pine Lake. His dad was working so much that he spent most of his visits with his grandparents. As a teenager, he didn't appreciate being in a quiet rural community or spending so much time with his grand-parents instead of his high school friends, but now he's grateful for those visits, and the community he found here. He especially likes quiet places like this that are tucked away from the summer tourists.

His grandmother would make a big breakfast of pancakes and eggs every morning and then he and his grandfather would ride their horses down the trail from the house and around their property. His grandfather would check the fences and stop at the orchard to check on the trees. Every time they did so, his grandfather would tell him about the big apple blight from long ago. They not only lost their entire harvest that year, but most of their trees as well. Ever since then, his grandfather had checked the trees daily to look for early signs of sickness so he could stop it from spreading through the entire orchard. While his grandfather checked the trees, Zach would climb them or throw rotten apples into the woods or pick a ripe apple off the tree for a snack.

He hadn't thought about his days in the orchard for years, and had wondered if it still looked the same. He's happy to find that for the most part, it does, although it's smaller than he remembered, and not as well maintained, showing some signs of neglect. His grandparents still own the farm, but they're much older now, and from the looks of the orchard, he's not able to care for things like he used to.

"Your grandfather sounds really special," Missy says.

"Yeah. I haven't thought about all the things we did together for a long time," Zach admits.

"Why do I get the feeling you haven't visited your grandparents since you've been back?" Missy asks.

Zach stares off into the trees as if they'd provide the words to express the complexity of his feelings about being back home.

"I haven't been great about staying in touch. I've really missed them. I guess I feel embarrassed. I'm not even sure I would know what to say; it's been too long."

"I'm sure they miss you and would love to see you," Missy says.

Zach shakes his head and tries to imagine what he would say on a visit to his grandparents. *Your grandson the felon is home* didn't sound like a great opening line.

Missy watches as Zach walks among the trees like his grandfather used to do. He would stop at a tree and seem to size it up, maybe taking note of how the tree hadn't been pruned, or looking for signs of sickness, like his grandfather taught him. She watches him kicking the remains of apples that lay on the ground. As far as she knows, this orchard isn't typically harvested. The apples just go to the deer and bear in the area. She smiles, enjoying watching how relaxed and at ease Zach seems to be, wandering among the trees. It's like he was made to work the land.

"I have something I think you're going to be excited about," she says when he finally settles back on their picnic blanket. "I cut us a few slices of the pie Ya-Ya made Catherine while you were cleaning up your tools." She reaches in her bag and pulls out a plastic container with two large slices of Ya-Ya's lemonade pie.

"Wow, this is amazing," Zach says, after he's taken a bite. "Do you sell this at the restaurant?" Zach asks, shoving another forkful into his mouth.

"No. Ya-Ya says the magic of her pies is the love. She makes each one with someone in mind and gives it to them as a gift. She feels that if she baked a large batch, the love would be missing."

"This is so good. You know people would pay for this," Zach says.

"All she wants is to bring smiles to those she loves."

"People would still smile if they paid for it. It's that good."

Missy just laughs, watching as Zach scrapes every bit of pie from the plastic container with his fork. Then he lies back on the blanket, tucking his hands under his head.

Missy rests her head on his shoulder. "You care about the business side of things too much," Missy teases.

"Maybe you care about it too little," Zach replies, pulling her into a hug.

Would I be less stressed if I thought about business like Zach does? she wonders.

"Your grandmother seems amazing."

"You have no idea." She sighs. "Most kids in their twenties wouldn't want to move in with their grandparents, but she made it so easy. She helped with Emma so I could finish school or just get a night's sleep. I don't know what I would do without her."

"Why'd you stay?"

"I didn't think I would settle here, but Ya-Ya needed my help with the Inn, and I guess I just fell even more in love with Pine Lake. Now I can't imagine living anywhere else."

Zach reaches for her hand. "I think being here with you makes it perfect," he says.

Missy smiles, giving his hand a gentle squeeze.

He rolls onto his side, props himself up on his elbow, and looks into her eyes. "Tell me where you saw yourself before you settled here."

She can't resist opening up to him; there is something inviting about the twinkle in his green eyes.

"Back in college, I always imagined myself working, in a stylish black suit and heels. I'm holding my briefcase and I've just landed in LA or Tokyo or some other big city. I'm making calls on my cell and rushing to an important meeting." She pauses to laugh at herself. "When I enter the room everyone stands, and someone brings me coffee. In the meeting, everyone listens to what I have to say. I don't know what I'm doing for a career, but in those dreams, I always felt so alive," she says.

Zach puts his arm around her. "I can see it, too. You'd be great."

"Well, all that is gone now, with Emma and the Inn." Missy sighs.

"Maybe it doesn't have to be," Zach says.

A tear escapes Missy's eye as the pressure she's been under for the past few years suddenly interrupts their picnic.

Zach gently wipes it away. He wraps his arm around her, and leaning in, his lips find hers. Her mouth parts, welcoming him, soft and tender. He holds her close, gently stroking her hair.

"It's not too late. You can still have dreams, you know," Zach says.

"Life had different plans for me," Missy says. "I don't have the luxury of big dreams anymore."

Missy rests her head on his chest, enjoying the peace of this moment with someone who seems to get her. She notices butterflies in a patch of wildflowers and watches as they dance from flower to flower.

"Look," Missy whispers, pointing at the butterflies.

Zach sits up on his elbows.

"They're so beautiful. I wonder what it feels like to be that free," she muses.

After relaxing in the orchard a bit longer, it's time to get back. They ride back along the wooded trail that connects to Catherine's property. Dismounting as Catherine's barn comes into view, they walk the horses back, holding hands.

Zach opens the gate to their fenced paddock, returning the horses for Catherine's stable hand to groom.

"I'll walk you out," Zach says.

Zach double-checks the door to be sure Catherine's house is locked up, and returns the hide-a-key to its secret spot under the front doormat. Zach puts his arm around Missy's shoulders as they walk up the path to her car. As she pulls out of the driveway, he raises his hand in a wave and watches her go.

Chapter 9

Catherine pulls into her garage and sets down a cardboard box in the middle of the mudroom before heading upstairs. She takes off her blouse, tossing it on the banister as she walks up the stairs, and unzips her skirt and steps out of it and drops it in her bedroom doorway. She walks over to her dresser and pulls out her swimsuit. She slips it on, along with board shorts, and heads out the back door and down to the lake.

Catherine had had little sleep after getting Zach from the police station, and it had been a long trip back and forth to the city, to close the sale on her house. She's looking forward to leaving her stress in the lake. Down by the water, she pulls her paddleboard off its rack and gently pushes off from shore. Exhaling deeply, she takes long smooth pulls on the paddle and glides across the water. Her board makes a lapping sound as she paddles down the length of her quiet cove.

Reaching the widest and busiest part of the lake, she steers toward a marshy section near the shore to stay out of the speedboat traffic. She sits down on her board and dangles her feet into the cool water to watch the sun sink behind the trees. She watches a fish pop up to the surface and leave a ripple of bubbles after it dives back below the surface. In the distance she can hear the buzz of a wakeboard boat long before she can see it. As it whizzes past her, she sees a young boy jumping the wake. Across the lake she sees a large pontoon anchored out, the family laughing and blasting upbeat summer tunes. She gives them a friendly wave. She loves the lengthening days of early summer.

Breathing in the fresh evening air, Catherine thinks back over her visit to sell her house in the city, the place she and Aleksandra had called home. The last tenants had moved out a few weeks ago, and the painters had put a fresh coat of neutral paint on the walls. It had felt both foreign and familiar at the same time.

Stepping into the living room, she'd felt the sunlight on her face from the large bay window. On the far end of the room, she ran her hand along the empty fireplace mantel. Closing her eyes, she could see each of the pictures that used to adorn it: the photo of herself, beaming and holding a swaddled Aleksandra on the day she was born; the photo of Aleksandra taking her first steps; Aleksandra, her hair in pigtails, waving as she stepped onto the bus for her first day of school.

She'd moved into the kitchen, pausing at the island. This room had truly been the heart of their home, filled with laughter and warmth. It was the place they'd gathered every day and caught up over meals. It was where they had baked cookies, cried over various dramas, and argued about homework. And it was the room where she'd first allowed herself to grieve the loss of her daughter.

Closing her eyes, Catherine had thought back on that night. The moments after the accident were a blur. She remembers sitting on the side of the road, cold and wet, and hearing the sirens. Later, in the hospital, her injuries were treated quickly while Aleksandra was rushed into surgery. She waited for hours, praying for an update, but when the doctor finally came out and told her that Aleksandra didn't make it through surgery, she wished he would take it back.

After saying good-bye to Aleksandra, she'd come home in a fog. She dropped her purse on the kitchen island and slid to the floor, curled up in a ball. Her tears flowed, and loud sobs racked her body until she had nothing left. She lay there motionless, feeling completely empty, and sleep took over.

The year that followed was a blur of darkness and emptiness. She had moved to Pine Lake, hoping that renovating her home on the lake would be a distraction from her grief, and while it wasn't, meeting Blake was. He had been a source of comfort—a reminder that life goes on, and that she needed to choose to keep on living even when she didn't want to. In Pine Lake she had found a reason to smile again. Falling in love with Blake meant a new chapter in her life, and she'd decided to stay in Pine Lake.

Relaxing now on her paddleboard, she reflects on her relationship with Blake. While staying in Pine Lake had felt like the right decision at the time, lately things between them had felt empty, and she wasn't so sure. Somehow selling the house in the city felt like losing a part of herself that she wasn't ready to let go of. She knows she should be grateful for the community she has built with Blake and Missy and Emma, but sometimes it feels like she's just going through the motions, sleepwalking through her life. She's waiting for something to happen, but she doesn't even know what it is. Something is missing and no one understands, not even her.

Despite her doubts, she'd signed her name on the settlement papers on the island and set her key on top. She'd taken a final look around before switching off the lights and closing the chapter on her time in the city.

Now, as she watches the sky fading from its bright blue to radiant shades of pink and orange, she can't help but wonder: *Did I just make the biggest mistake of my life?*

She stands on her board and paddles up the quiet cove to her dock.

Back inside the house, she opens a cardboard box and gently pulls out the birdfeeder Aleksandra had made for Mother's Day, in elementary school. Tracing over the faded designs Aleksandra had painted so many years ago transports Catherine back to that celebration. She remembers them laughing together in the kitchen while making blueberry French toast. After their brunch, Aleksandra surprised her with this gift. Catherine had torn off the paper and cried as Aleksandra showed her the round sun with its happy face shining down on the mama and daughter stick figures, holding hands. Before cleaning up, they'd hung the feeder outside the kitchen window so they could watch the birds anytime they were cooking together.

Tracing her finger over the faded designs, she carries the feeder out onto her back deck and hangs it on an empty hook outside her kitchen window.

Chapter 10

Missy steps out onto the deck and looks at the buzz of vendors who have set up on the back lawn for the Slice of Summer Picnic. She heads over to the grandstand and adjusts the red, white, and blue balloons, and then crosses to the food tent to check in with the catering team, to make sure everything's ready.

Hearing her name, Missy looks up and sees Ya-Ya coming toward her. Barely five feet tall, Ya-Ya's become round from age, and a few too many slices of pie.

Missy feels Ya-Ya's leathery hand slip into hers.

"It's lovely," Ya-Ya says, her eyes welling up with tears as she takes it all in.

"I don't know how you're never stressed."

"At my age, you know life always has a way of working itself out,"
she whispers, giving Missy's hand a gentle squeeze. As they hug, Missy
lets out a breath she didn't even realize she'd been holding.

"I just want it to be absolutely perfect."

"And it will be. Now go—enjoy." Ya-Ya kisses her forehead, leaving
her trademark red lipstick print.

Missy heads over to the grandstand and takes the microphone
from its stand, lightly tapping it to make sure it's on. Looking out
over the crowd, she feels her heart pounding in her chest. She smiles
and takes a breath before she begins.

"Welcome! I want to thank you all for joining us here today for
our sixty-fifth Slice of Summer Picnic," Missy announces, and cuts the
symbolic ribbon across the grandstand. "In a few minutes, our youth
fishing tournament will begin. If you want to participate, sign up at
the table over there and then meet down by the dock for instructions."
Missy motions toward the sign-up table near the edge of the lake.

Stepping down from the grandstand, Missy is almost knocked
over as Emma runs to greet her with a hug.

"Mommy, I want to do the fishing tournament," Emma whines,
tugging at her hand.

"Baby, I have to welcome all the guests and keep things running
for the picnic," Missy says. She looks around, trying to figure out how
she can help Emma and still do her job, wishing there was some way
for her to be in two places at once.

At that moment Zach walks over and wraps her in a hug. "Hey,
there, woman of the hour!"

"Zach can do the fishing tournament with me," Emma says nonchalantly.

"Oh, I don't know that Zach wants to do that," Missy whispers to
her daughter, catching Zach's eye.

Smiling back at Missy, Zach kneels down to Emma's level. "I would
be happy to fish with you, Emma," Zach says. He leads Emma toward

the sign-up table and writes their names on the form, picking up a plastic bowl of night crawlers.

"Do you know how to put the worm on your hook?" Zach asks.

"Ewww," Emma squeals.

Zach kneels next to her, unearthing a night crawler from the dirt in the bowl, and shows her how to slide it onto his hook. He guides her as she fishes another one out of the dirt and baits her hook. With their lines ready, they wade into a shallow section of the water near the shore and he helps her cast her line and reel the excess back in.

"My dad taught me to fish here when I was just about your age," Zach tells Emma.

"I don't have a dad," Emma says matter-of-factly.

Zach nods, thinking how often he felt left out of father-and-son activities when he was in Minnesota with his mom.

"Actually, I do. He's just looking for buried treasure," Emma says.

"Oh?" Zach says, unsure of how to respond.

"Yeah, he'll be back when he finds it," she says.

Zach nods in agreement.

"Have you ever caught a fish?" she asks.

"I have. I even won the tournament here a few times. I'll have to show you the photos hanging inside."

"When I grow up, I'm going to be a mermaid pirate so I can play with all the fish every day," Emma says.

"I think you have something on your line. Let's reel it in and check," Zach says, and helps her reel in her line.

"I got a fish! I got a fish!" she shouts.

"Grab the bucket and let's take it over to the table to get it measured!" Zach tousles her hair and waves Missy over to see Emma's catch.

"I think we have a natural here," Zach says, showing Missy the bucket that contains Emma's fish.

They walk over to measure her catch, and the official declares Emma the official winner of the sixty-fifth Summer Slice fishing tournament. Emma collects her fish shaped trophy and Zach scoops her up and spins her around. As they head back to the lawn, Zach points out a butterfly dancing along a patch of purple daisies. While Missy watches the butterfly, he picks a few daisies and hands them to Emma. "Give these to your mama," Zach whispers.

"Mama, Zach found these for you," she says, smiling.

Missy bends down so her daughter can place one of the flowers in her hair.

"How do I look?" she asks, winking at Zach.

"Beautiful, Mama," Emma says, before running back to the lake to splash in the shallow water.

"Be careful, Emma," Missy calls after her.

"She's adorable," Zach remarks.

"She has her moments."

"The picnic is amazing. You really did a great job," Zach says, grabbing her hand.

Missy smiles in agreement, feeling proud of herself as she takes in the crowd on the lawn. Guests near the stage are dancing and singing along with the band, the food tent is busy with guests getting hot dogs and hamburgers, and cheers erupt from the cornhole tournament.

She'd been scared about hosting the first Slice of Summer Picnic since Granddaddy had passed, but it had turned out to be a huge success. She never would have gotten it all done if it hadn't been for Catherine and Blake's help.

"This may be one of the best turnouts we've ever had," Missy says, beaming with pride.

She watches as Emma splashes along the shoreline, chasing a butterfly. Being able to enjoy moments like this made all of the stress worthwhile.

"Come on in, Emma, and get something to eat," Missy calls.

The three start off for the food tent, where they're intercepted by a reporter.

"Excuse me," the reporter says, stopping Missy. "Can I get a photo of you with our fishing champion for the paper?" she asks.

Zach steps back and the reporter says, "All three of you get closer together now. Come on, I want to get the whole family."

"Oh no, we aren't—" Missy starts to say.

"Say cheese," the reporter says, snapping a photo of the three of them as Zach leans in, wrapping his arms around Missy and Emma.

"Do you have time for a few questions to go along with the story?" the reporter asks.

"Go ahead," Zach says, encouraging her. "This is your moment. I'll take Emma to get a hot dog and her face painted."

Missy watches Zach hoist Emma onto his shoulders and jog over to the food tent, weaving around like he's an airplane.

"Why don't you tell me what the Inn means to the community?" the reporter asks.

Missy pauses to reflect, taking in the crowd of familiar faces, young and old.

"Well, my grandparents started the Inn the year they got married, and it's been part of the community for sixty-five years. It's a place where families can create memories that last for generations, and I want the Inn to continue doing so for years to come," she says, smiling.

"When do we get to learn your grandmother's secret recipe for lemonade pie?" the reporter asks.

Missy laughs. "Her pie is almost as legendary as she is, but even I don't know her secret. I think she's planning to take that with her when she goes."

As the interview concludes, Missy smiles, taking in the success of the picnic. The parking lot is full of cars, as is the overflow lot across the street from the Inn. On the back lawn the guests are laughing and dancing along with the band.

Missy hears Emma talking with a woman nearby.

"Arrgghh, look at my eye patch!" Emma says, having gotten her face painted like a pirate.

The woman moves back to make sure Emma's face paint and sticky hands don't get on her short white sundress. "Yes, very nice," she says warily, scanning the lawn for a familiar face.

"Are you bothering this lady, Emma?" Missy asks.

"I was just showing her my eye patch," Emma says before running off to play with her friends.

"I'm Missy," she says, shaking the hand of the unfamiliar guest. "Thank you for coming."

"I'm looking for Zach Hartmann," the woman replies. "Do you know him?"

"Yes. I think I know where he is. Come with me," Missy says. "Are you new in town?" Missy asks, watching the woman teeter-totter across the grass, trying not to lose her stiletto heels in the soft ground.

"Just here to surprise Zach. I'm Tracey. How do I look?"

Missy takes in her outfit and opens her mouth to reply, but Tracey continues. "I know it's a hard time for him right now. He's so stressed about his upcoming trial. I mean, I guess I would be stressed, too, if I was facing a huge fine and years of jail time, like he is."

"So, you're a friend of Zach's?" Missy asks.

Without pausing to answer Missy's question, Tracey rambles on. "But I love him, and I will stand beside him, no matter what."

"I'm sure he'll be very happy to see you," Missy says, not sure what to say.

Missy spots Catherine chatting with her parents near the gazebo. She watches as Catherine's dad casually drapes his arm around his daughter's shoulder. She feels a twinge of jealousy, wishing her parents doted on her like Catherine's do.

"I'm going to get a refill. Can I get you anything?" Harold asks, bringing Missy back to reality.

"I'm sorry, are we intruding on family time here?" Missy asks.

Before anyone can answer, Tracey asks, "Have you seen Zach?"

"I think he's getting a drink. I'll send him over," Harold says.

"Missy will agree with me. Isn't that gazebo the perfect spot for Blake and Catherine's wedding?" Betsy says.

"Sure, it would be lovely," Missy agrees.

"How much longer are you going to make me wait to see you walk down the aisle?" Betsy asks.

Catherine looks at the gazebo, picturing Blake smiling beneath it, surrounded by purple and white roses, watching her approach. She feels tempted by the fantasy wedding, but then she reminds herself of the reality of their relationship.

"Good grief, Mom! It's not like you're dying," Catherine says, patting her mother's shoulder to calm her down.

Blake walks over and gives Betsy a hug. "What are my two favorite ladies gossiping about?"

"Mom was admiring your gazebo. You did an amazing job," Catherine says.

"Yes, the gazebo is gorgeous," Betsy says, "but I was saying, don't you think it's time to make it official? This is a perfect spot." Betsy winks.

"Mom!" Catherine exclaims.

"I'm just saying, summer weddings are so romantic. Don't you all agree?" Betsy asks.

Blake glances sideways at Catherine, who is sipping her wine and not meeting his gaze.

"You know, Betsy, I don't think it's the right time for us," Blake offers.

"I think Zach and I will get married at sunset," Tracey pipes up.

"So you're Zach's girlfriend?" Missy asks.

Blake suddenly spots Zach. "Son, we're over here," Blake calls out, waving Zach over.

Fantastic, Zach thinks to himself. They haven't spoken since he was detained after the bar fight, and now his dad's doing his usual clueless-dad act, pretending nothing is wrong. After thirty-two years of parenting, he still doesn't know how to have a real conversation.

Taking a deep breath, he offers the group a half wave and clenched smile as he makes his way toward them.

"Missy, want to join me for some iced tea?" Catherine asks, staring into her full glass of wine.

"Nope. I want to stay right here and get to know Zach's friend," Missy says, crossing her arms.

"Zach, buddy, you didn't mention that you were inviting a friend," Blake says.

Zach chokes on a sip of beer as he notices that Tracey is part of the group.

"That's because I didn't invite a friend," Zach says pointedly.

"Surprise!" Tracey squeals, hurling herself across the lawn and hugging Zach, who stands frozen, his arms glued to his sides.

"What are you doing here?" Zach asks.

"Aren't you excited to see me?" Tracey asks Zach, still wrapping her arms around him.

"I don't know about everyone else, but I sure am surprised," Missy says, eyes squinted at Zach.

"Oh my, honey, you seem to have forgotten your manners," Tracey says, nudging Zach in the ribs and laughing.

Zach fidgets with his beer can, looking down at the grass.

"Am I missing something?" Blake asks.

"This is Zach's girlfriend, Tracey. Isn't she adorable?" Missy says.

Catherine spits out her wine.

"Tracey's not my girlfriend," Zach says.

"And apparently Zach is facing a big trial where he faces possible prison time," Missy adds.

Blake swings around to stare at his son.

"It's a bit more complicated than that," Zach says.

Missy laughs. "Isn't that what he always says—that it's complicated? Let me break it down for you. Tracey, this is Betsy, Catherine's mom, who thinks it's high time her daughter got married. Here we have Catherine, who is annoyed at her boyfriend's lack of commitment. Which brings us to Blake, Zach's dad, who is ashamed that his son is being charged with a felony. And I'm Missy, the single mom Zach's been hitting on since escaping all the lies he left back in Minnesota. Enjoy the party." With that, she storms off to the Inn.

Tracey's mouth hangs open, speechless, as her eyes dart from person to person. She tucks a strand of hair behind her ear and straightens her shoulders and smiles.

"It's such a pleasure to meet everyone," she says.

Everyone just glares back at her in silence.

Blake looks at Zach, his eyes cold and angry. "Zach, what is she talking about?"

"Don't worry about it. This doesn't involve you," Zach deflects.

"How could you come back here and not tell me what's going on?" Blake asks.

"What are you talking about? When have we ever talked about anything more than the weather or football?" Zach asks.

"I think felony charges are the kind of thing you might want to mention," Blake says.

"Whatever," Zach says, rolling his eyes.

"Don't make this about me. You're a grown man, and it's time for you to get your life together," Blake shouts.

"You have no idea what you're talking about. I have it under control," Zach replies.

"I think I have a few more years of experience than you," Blake insists.

"How's that working out for you? The woman you love looks pretty angry to me. Did you let her down like you did me?" Zach says.

"That's between me and Catherine," Blake snaps.

"Of course it is. You need to focus on my shortcomings to take the attention off your own," Zach snaps back.

"Nice attitude. How about you get serious for once and call a lawyer and fix your mess?" Blake says.

As Zach storms off, Blake calls after him, "Oh, and make things right with Missy."

Blake turns to Catherine. "Did you know about all this?"

"This was Zach's news to share with you, not mine," Catherine states.

"You knew about all of this, and you didn't tell me?" he shouts.

"Maybe you should ask yourself why I knew before you," Catherine says, stepping back.

The sky has grown dark and thunder claps shake the ground.

Catherine watches the gray storm clouds rolling in as she hurries to her car to drive home.

Chapter 11

The picnic guests have all gone home and the band is loading up the last of their equipment. A staff member is grabbing the balloons and moving them inside before the storm starts.

Zach jogs across the lawn, searching for Missy. Raindrops begin to fall, and with each one that hits his head, his dad's words ring in his ears: "Fix your mess." *What does he think I've been doing?* Zach thinks.

He sees Missy on the deck and watches as she picks up discarded paper plates and cups that guests had set down and forgotten about, stopping along the way to chat with someone. He can't hear what they are saying, but he can see the warmth pouring out of her in the way she throws her head back, laughing at the story they are sharing, how her face lights up as she smiles, and the gentle way she touches the guest's forearm and giggles.

His breath catches in his throat. *Why didn't I just tell her about everything sooner?* He knows it's because he was worried she wouldn't like him if she knew the truth about who he really is.

Zach climbs the steps up to the deck and joins Missy in picking up trash, quietly thinking over all the things he wants to say. Somehow he can't seem to get any words to come out of his mouth. Like a peace offering, he brings a handful of trash to put in the trash bag Missy's holding, and is met with a glare.

"Can we talk?" Zach asks.

Shoving the trash bag at Zach, she snaps, "I think it's you who needs to start talking."

Zach picks up more trash from the table and adds it to the bag before sitting down and rubbing his temples.

"Tracey and I are over," he starts.

"I don't think she got the memo," Missy says, rolling her eyes. She balls up the plastic tablecloth from the table and throws it at Zach.

Zach adds it to the bag and then ties it up, grabbing a clean towel and disinfectant spray to wash down the table. In silence he methodically cleans, considering what more to say.

Zach has never known the level of love and acceptance that Missy shares with those in her life. Growing up, he always felt love was doled out frugally, in exchange for some good deed he had done, like getting a satisfactory report card, or earning his degree, or achieving success with a big deal. It felt like collecting tickets at the arcade that you could use for the big prize, but no matter how hard you tried, you never had enough for the prize you really wanted.

With Missy it's different. It's like her smile, her eyes, her hugs offer a free-flowing supply of love. It feels like she always has more than enough to give.

Setting down the towel, he joins Missy at the edge of the covered deck, where she's straightening the row of Adirondack chairs. He takes her hands in his and invites her to sit down with him. Looking into her eyes, he sees they are red, probably from crying over the pain that he caused.

"I feel so stupid," he says.

Missy looks away, her eyes holding back the tears that threaten to spill down her cheeks.

Zach leans back in his chair, trying to calm his pounding heart.

"I wish I knew what I could say to make this right."

Closing his eyes, he thinks back on his life, watching it in his mind like a movie. He sees himself working three jobs to pay for his undergrad tuition. Working his internship during the day and bartending at night to pay for his MBA. Working seventy to eighty hours a week, chasing the next big deal to land the promotion.

Zach opens his eyes and looks out over the lake, still not saying a word.

It's not just about Tracey, he thinks. *Maybe it's realizing that I have spent my whole life trying to prove myself to the world. Trying to get them to see how great I am, because I didn't believe it myself.*

Sitting here now with Missy, he realizes that when he is with her, he feels like enough. It's the first time he's ever felt like he can just be still and enjoy the moment. He doesn't feel like he has to prove how great he is.

"I didn't know this was possible," Zach finally says. "When I came to Pine Lake . . ." His voice catches in his throat and he pauses to catch his breath. "What I mean is, Tracey is part of the worst thing that has ever happened to me in my life, and when I got here and met you, I guess I felt like maybe I could leave all of that behind. Maybe I could finally be me."

Missy leans back in her chair, considering his words before turning toward him.

"But you can't just leave your past behind. Life doesn't work like that," she says.

Zach nods, knowing she is right, while also not sure what that means for them.

"I didn't want to be defined by that when we'd only just met. I really like you and I'm not just a lawsuit."

"Well, I hope you can understand why I'm shocked and hurt that you kept this from me."

"My lawyer is handling things with the case, but beyond that, I'm not sure who I am without my career. It's all I know—all that I'm good at," he finally says.

Missy turns towards him, gently touching his arm. "I guess you need to stop running away and start figuring things out."

The rain starts to fall, and Missy leaves to go check on Ya-Ya and Emma.

Zach sits alone on the covered deck looking out over the lake.

He knows he doesn't want Tracey; their relationship doesn't compare to what he has found with Missy. He didn't even know a woman like Missy existed. She is kind and loving and smart and funny. He loves how she always gets down on Emma's level or picks her up when talking to her. She is so gentle and patient with Ya-Ya, making sure she takes her medicine and doesn't do too much. She takes care of everyone while running the Inn. The hotel business is known for being relentless and unforgiving, yet she is always smiling and talking with the guests, making it look so easy. She is a natural, and doesn't even realize how talented and amazing she is, which just makes him love her even more.

He has never been afraid to lose a woman before, maybe because he has never cared enough, or maybe there's never been someone this special, who mattered so much to him.

Maybe I never actually loved anyone before Missy, he thinks. *And now that I have truly figured out what love feels like, I may lose her forever.*

Zach's thoughts turn to what Missy said—that he's running away from his problems. He has never been one to shy away from a challenge, so this time shouldn't be any different.

He takes out his phone to text Scott to make arrangements for a flight back home.

Emma bounds through the screen door and wraps her arms around his legs in a big hug. "I love you, Zach!" she says, and then runs back inside.

Zach sees Missy through the window, chatting with her guests. He wishes he could pull her in for one more hug and feel her arms loop around his waist and her head against his chest. He imagines the smell of her hair as he kisses the top of her head.

I will fix this, he says, in a silent promise to himself and to Missy.

Chapter 12

Zach texts Tracey and asks her to meet him at the old diner in town, to talk. He sends her the address, and arrives a few minutes early.

Kicking the gravel in the parking lot as he waits, he thinks, *Aren't I already dealing with enough without Tracey creating drama?*

Tracey pulls in and parks her car on the other side of the small lot.

He remembers the first time he saw her. He was just twenty-one years old that summer afternoon when he boarded Mr. Anderson's sailboat for the first time. He couldn't take his eyes off her. She was tall and slender, with long auburn hair and dark brown eyes. He remembers how their eyes locked. He watched from afar while she was telling a story to her girlfriends. They hung on every word she said and laughed generously at her jokes. It was clear they all wanted to be her, and if he was honest with himself, maybe he did, too.

It was four years after that initial meeting before they finally became a couple but over the years, he watched her perform like this at every black-tie gala and charity dinner they attended. She always knew how to work the room, smiling politely and making small talk, and she never forgot a face. She made sure he met all the right people and got all the right introductions. When they weren't making the rounds of the social circuit, they spent their summer weekends sailing at her family's house on Lake Harriet and their winters skiing at her dad's chalet in the Rocky Mountains.

He watches her climb out of her car now, offering her a wave and a forced smile. A knot forms in his stomach as he realizes he barely recognizes her. Of course, he's still familiar with the way she flicks her hair off her shoulders and how her hips sway when she walks, but with each step she takes, he feels like something has changed, and it isn't her. The past week in Pine Lake changed him. He feels somehow different now.

As she approaches, he opens his mouth to greet her but nothing comes out. He immediately feels stupid and shoves his hands in his pockets.

Tracey leans against the rear bumper of his car. Pulling her cardigan tighter around her chest, she joins him in kicking the gravel beneath her feet and they stand there silently for what feels like an eternity.

"I was thinking about giving you a piece of my mind," Zach says.

"I thought about doing the same thing."

Zach watches a family load into their minivan, one kid fussing with the red balloon tied to his wrist while another one cries as his exhausted mom tries to buckle him into his car seat.

"I guess I shouldn't have come," Tracey says.

"No, I probably should have told you what I was doing here."

"In all the years I've known you, you have never talked about Pine Lake."

"You never asked," Zach says a little too abruptly.

116

Tracey nods her head in agreement, "I guess I could sense that you never wanted to talk about things with your dad. Why did you come here?" Tracey asks.

Zach's anger boils to the surface as he thinks about how her dad was the one who orchestrated the deal that had landed him in this mess. Taking a deep breath, he clenches and unclenches his fists, ignoring her question.

After a moment, Tracey says, "I thought I had the perfect life, and then one day I woke up and found out it was all a lie. My perfect family and perfect life are gone. My mom can't get out of bed. I don't even know where my dad is. And then you left."

"All I ever wanted was to be just like your dad."

"It all feels so unfair," Tracey says.

Zach nods, and goes back to aimlessly kicking the gravel.

Tracey takes Zach's hand in hers.

"I know I'm not going through the same thing you are, with the court charges and all, but my life was stolen from me, too. I'm alone and I'm scared. Do you get that?"

"I do," Zach says.

"I miss you," Tracey says, her chin quivering. "I always thought we were going to have an amazing life together, and now . . . I don't know."

Zach thinks back on the seven years he's shared with Tracey. From the outside they looked like the ideal match. She had certainly checked all the boxes for what he'd thought he wanted in a wife—beautiful and smart, and they got along well—but their connection didn't compare with how he feels when he's with Missy—which is truly himself. He smiles, thinking how Missy is always freezing, even when wearing a sweater in the early summer sun; how adorable it is that she has to have her black coffee in the same pink mug every morning, and her unsweetened tea in the same red cup every afternoon.

How did he not know any of Tracey's little quirks?

"I think I did, too, but this time apart has shown me that we aren't right for each other," Zach says.

Tracey nods.

"I'm sorry I haven't been there for you," Zach says. "To be honest, I've been so preoccupied with all my legal stuff, I didn't even think about how hard it was on you, with your dad gone."

"I'm sorry I wasn't there for you, either."

"I don't know if we've ever really been there for each other," he says.

"With my dad, I always felt taken care of. I didn't have to worry about anything. When I met you, I think I just expected the same from you, too," Tracey says.

"I know what you mean," Zach says. "You're wonderful, Tracey, but—"

Tracey raises her hand to stop him before he can finish. "I know." A tear escapes her eye and she quickly wipes it away.

Zach gives Tracey a long hug before she heads back to her car.

She climbs in and gives him a wave, and he watches until he can no longer see her taillights in the distance.

Chapter 13

*C*atherine drives home from the picnic on autopilot, replaying her fight with Blake in her head. She feels the heaviness of things between them. Everything has been off, from fights about their future to things with Zach. They just don't seem to be on the same page about anything. When she gets home and turns off the ignition, all she feels is exhausted. *What am I even fighting for?* she wonders.

She heads inside and drops her purse on the kitchen counter. She opens the sliding door to the deck, allowing the storm winds to blow through her house. *Fresh air will clear my mind*, she thinks, and heads outside for a walk down the country lane.

The storm has just passed, leaving the air cool and crisp. The only sound she can hear is the thud of her feet. She takes a deep breath, smelling the pine scent from the freshly fallen needles carpeting the ground, and feels her shoulders begin to relax. Off to her right, the sun is setting behind the tall loblolly pines, painting the sky vibrant shades of pink and orange. And on her left, the full moon is rising high above the grove of dense pine trees, casting a soft glow on the quiet street.

At the end of the lane, she turns around and heads back to her house. She can hear the muffled sounds of a summer barbecue coming from the neighbor's patio, the quiet chatter, an uproar of laughter, and the rumblings of classic rock on their stereo.

Once inside, Catherine opens a bottle of crisp white wine and settles in on the chaise lounge on her back patio. Adjusting her blanket and sipping her wine, she thinks about all the things she wishes she had said to Blake at the picnic.

She isn't trying to take Blake's place as Zach's parent, or compete with him for Zach's love and attention. She's simply trying to be supportive of Zach. She wishes Blake would understand this.

The sound of tires crunching gravel in the driveway makes her heart pound, and her stomach does flip-flops. Will Blake join her on the patio?

Hearing the sliding door open, she feels the knot in her stomach clench tighter.

When Zach steps out onto the patio, she exhales loudly.

"Oh, it's you," she says.

"Wow, thanks. Hello to you, too," Zach teases.

"I'm sorry. I thought maybe it was your dad."

"So he's not here?" Zach asks.

Catherine shakes her head and takes another sip of her wine.

"I'm heading back to Minnesota in the morning," Zach says.

"That seems kind of sudden," she says. "What's happening with your case? And don't give me that 'I don't know.'"

Zach laughs. "Well, it's something like that," he says.

He grabs some logs from the stack nearby and starts a fire in the fire pit, then settles into the chair beside Catherine.

"I want to hear the whole story—and I do mean the whole story. Don't leave out a single detail," she says in her mom voice. "Grab yourself a beer or some wine and then tell me everything."

"It's a beautiful night. Usually with a full moon, you can't see so many stars," Zach says when he comes back out with a beer.

After taking a minute to study the stars and collect his thoughts, he fills her in on how he first met Mr. Anderson, his internship during business school, his mentorship when he was just starting out—how they started doing deals together regularly, and then, the FBI raid on his office, when they seized his files.

"This sounds serious," Catherine says, trying to process everything he'd just shared.

Zach rubs his temples, unsure of how to explain. Of course, he's worried about having to pay a fine, and the possibility of prison time, but it's more than that. This is his life. These charges mean the end of his career and his dreams of finding love, marriage, and a family. What would even be left to live for?

Unable to think of the right words, Zach shrugs and shakes his head.

"Did you notice anything wrong with the deal?" Catherine asks.

"For the longest time, I told myself there weren't any signs, but in the time I've been here, it's like my mind is clearer. I'm starting to think of things I didn't notice before."

"Like what?" Catherine probes.

Zach grabs the fireplace poker and shifts the logs until the fire roars to life again, warming their faces. He closes his eyes to collect his thoughts, then shares with Catherine a few of the moments that seemed unusual.

Like why after forty-five years in business Mr. Anderson had left his longtime auditor, loyal friend, and golf buddy, Robert, and hired a first-year partner to handle things? Why had he brushed off Zach's questions? Mr. Anderson had seemed edgy, micromanaging every aspect of the process, where he'd typically been hands off, letting Zach and the team handle things.

Catherine sits up straighter in her chair and nods, listening to Zach.

"The numbers started to look sketchy, too, but I just hoped that once the merger was complete, sales would take off, the meal kits would fly off the shelves, and everything would work out. I didn't think that people would get hurt."

Zach is silent for a moment, then continues.

"This was the first time I'd ever felt so relieved when a deal was done. I deposited the commission in my savings account, but then, for some reason, I couldn't bring myself to touch it."

"And now you can't," Catherine says.

"You're not wrong." Zach laughs.

Zach stands up and paces in front of the fire, exhaling a deep breath and taking a long drink of his beer.

"I can't believe I brokered a deal that is causing so many people to lose so much money. Families have lost their retirement savings, or money for their kids' college tuition, all because of me. I feel so guilty."

"You're being way too hard on yourself, Zach. You didn't do this deal on your own. The court will surely see that."

"I should have trusted myself when things felt off. I should have spoken up. I sold innocent people out, and for what?"

Catherine stands, gently placing her hand on Zach's arm. "Of course, looking back, you see things you could have done differently, but beating yourself up isn't going to help. All you can do now is learn from this experience and share what you know in court. You can do your best to try and make things right."

"I told myself I didn't know what I was looking at, but deep down, I knew. I just chose to look the other way," Zach says, crushing his beer can flat.

"There was a whole team involved," says Catherine. "Why are you the only one being held responsible? What about the auditors, or Mr. Anderson? What evidence does your lawyer have?"

Zach just shakes his head in disbelief.

"Do you have a forensic accountant reviewing the financials?" Catherine asks.

Zach shrugs. "I don't know."

"This is what I do. I'm a CPA, and I specialize in forensic accounting. Tell your lawyer I am coming to Minnesota with you tomorrow. We need to go over everything you have."

"No, it's okay. I don't want to drag you into this, too," Zach says.

"Look, it's no trouble. I want to do this for you."

Back in his room at his dad's house, Zach sits down on his bed and traces the drawing Emma had made for him, in brightly colored crayons. The stick figures had big red smiles and were holding hands. The round yellow sun was also wearing a big red smile.

Dropping his head in his hands, he wonders how he let everything get so messed up—first, his career, and now, Missy. He wishes he could run over to the Inn and make her understand. He would beg for her forgiveness and tell her how ashamed he feels, to have let her down—how it will never happen again. But he knows he has to go home and settle the lawsuit if he's ever going to be able to look her in the eyes again.

Checking the time, he climbs into bed, turns off the light, and tries to get some sleep before he heads back to Minnesota.

Chapter 14

*I*t's late as Blake pulls into his driveway. As his headlights illuminate the darkness of the house, he realizes he's not ready to go inside. He puts the car in reverse and drifts down the driveway, continuing along the road until he finds himself in an old familiar spot. He parks the car in the empty driveway and allows the memories to wash over him.

On summer nights like this one, Zach's mom, Jenny, would sneak out after her parents fell asleep. Jenny and Blake would jump from the rope swing and swim under the stars until they were exhausted, and then curl up under blankets on the dock. They would lie on their backs and Jenny would point out the constellations and they would wish on shooting stars.

Now the house was abandoned, the dock a rusty heap in the overgrown yard.

Blake wanders through the brush and takes a seat on a rock at the water's edge. He pulls out his phone and unlocks it, then puts it away. Pulling it out again, he looks up Jenny in his contact list.

Should he call her? Probably not a great idea.

Still, outside of Catherine, Jenny knows him better than anyone else.

They had been young when they fell in love, but their love was still real. He'd thought they would go from being high school sweethearts to graduating college together and raising their family, here on the edge of Pine Lake. When she'd told him she was pregnant with Zach, he hadn't suggested getting married. He'd just promised to support her in any way he could. When she said her parents were relocating to Minnesota and she was going with them, he stood by his promise. She was only eighteen, and she needed her mom more than she needed him. He had understood, but still, watching her pull away with her parents thirty-three years ago was the hardest thing he had ever done.

He sits down on a rock where the old dock used to be, rolls up the legs of his jeans, and dips his feet in the water.

He wonders if he made the wrong decision all those years ago. Certainly, Zach thinks so. Maybe that was one of those times you hear about, when women say one thing and mean another. Maybe he was supposed to race across the country and make some grand romantic gesture—propose to Jenny, promise to never leave her side—but they were both so young. At the time, he'd felt like that would have just complicated an already complicated time. So he gave her space and worked night and day to build his business, and sent her money to take care of Zach.

He missed Zach's first steps, his first day of school—all those birthdays and graduations. He can't ever go back to those years, or acquire those memories. All he'd ever wanted was to make sure Zach was taken care of. He had given up his dream of studying to be an architect. He'd given up on finding love. With all the hours he worked, everything he did was for Zach.

126

But somehow, it still wasn't enough.

Looking at the full moon's bright reflection on the lake, he makes a decision. He presses the call button, and seconds later, he hears Jenny's warm, familiar voice pick up.

"Blake, is that you?" he hears her say.

"I'm sorry it's so late. I shouldn't have called."

"No, it's fine. Are you okay?"

Blake moves his feet back and forth in the water, gazing out over the lake and exhaling audibly.

"I just had a fight with Zach. I told him to grow up and stop running away from his problems," Blake admits.

"Oh."

"I know. He just pushes all my buttons," Blake says.

"He's under a lot of stress right now."

"I wouldn't know. He doesn't tell me anything," Blake says.

"How could he?" she asks. After a brief silence, Jenny says, "There are protesters downtown every day. He had the media camped out on his front lawn. Some people threw eggs at his house and spray-painted graffiti on his garage. People are angry. Why do you think he went to Pine Lake?"

"I had no idea."

"Of course you didn't, but maybe you could have asked him before jumping to conclusions and criticizing."

"You were always better at this than me."

"I'm no better than you," Jenny says gently. "I just showed up."

"What's done is done. I can't change it now."

"You're right, but you can change what you do next."

"Thanks, Jenny," Blake says.

He ends the call and tucks his phone back into his pocket. Lying back, he looks up at the night sky and tries to make out the constellations.

Chapter 15

*A*fter a sleepless night, tossing and turning and replaying her conversation with Zach in her head, Missy drags herself out of bed. Rubbing her eyes, she reaches for the nearest shirt and pants she can find and shuffles to the kitchen. She grabs her favorite pink mug and pours herself a large cup of coffee. She nods a silent good morning to the kitchen staff and heads down the hall to her office. She needs to review the upcoming week's reservations and cash flow projection reports Catherine set up in her system.

A few minutes later, Ya-Ya knocks softly on her open office door to announce herself. When Missy looks up, she says, "Come with me."

Looking at the mess of papers on her desk, Missy wants to protest, but she knows that Ya-Ya isn't actually asking. She takes Ya-Ya's hand and follows her into their private kitchen.

Ya-Ya instructs her to get out the mixing bowl and measuring cups while she starts pulling milk and butter from the refrigerator and sugar and graham crackers from the pantry, all the ingredients for her lemonade pie.

"I never told you this, but shortly after your granddaddy and I started going steady, I found out he was making eyes at another girl," Ya-Ya says.

"What?" Missy gasps in shock. She never thought of Granddaddy as anything but loyal to Ya-Ya. He'd always been an honest, hard-working family man.

Ya-Ya breaks graham crackers into the food processor and pulverizes them into fine crumbs for the crust and then begins her story.

"Back then Granddaddy was working for his father at the bank, a fact Martha Miller didn't miss. One afternoon, Martha went into the bank and told him how confused she was, and asked for his help to sort out her bank book. She was flustered and started crying, but that didn't bother your grandfather." Ya-Ya pauses and smiles, remembering. "He was always so patient with customers, and such a great teacher. He took his time and carefully explained how to use her bank book to record and balance all of her transactions. She made notes but was still wiping away tears as he finished, and he suggested they go to the soda fountain to cheer her up.

"Well, your grandfather's little sister, Betty—she was my best friend—and I were already in Friend's Five and Dime, picking out some sweets, when they walked in. Martha had her arm looped through your grandfather's as they slid onto two stools at the counter and ordered their sodas. We watched as she laughed and gently put her hand on his arm, leaning into him, asking about the latest movies playing. I burst into tears and dropped all my candy. I ran out of the store with Betty chasing after me. Your grandfather saw us as we passed the counter, and he called after us, but I didn't stop or look back. I couldn't watch them together."

"You must have been so heartbroken," Missy says, as she pours the melted butter Ya-Ya measured out over the graham cracker crumbs and mixes them with her hands, hanging on every word.

Ya-Ya shakes her head, seemingly transported back in time.

"I was devastated," she says, slowly pressing the crumbs into the pie dish before continuing her story.

"Betty and I ran all the way home from the Five and Dime and I threw myself down on my bed, crying. Betty headed to her home for dinner and my mom tried to convince me to come downstairs, but I wouldn't leave my room. Later that evening, your grandfather came by, and with some coaxing, I agreed to talk to him."

"Why did you agree to talk to him?" Missy asks.

"Oh, I think it was only so I could give him a piece of my mind," Ya-Ya says with a hearty laugh. "But as we sat on the front porch swing, sipping our sweet tea, I felt less angry," she continues.

"Initially, we just there in silence, each of us probably waiting for the other to begin. Finally he moved closer and took my hand in his. He explained what really happened with Martha, and that he didn't realize she was flirting with him. Before you say I was naive, you need to understand that your grandfather was a real looker back in the day. Martha certainly wasn't the first girl to set her cap for him, or the last, but as we sat on that swing for hours that night, he told me about all the dreams he had for our life together."

"I know why you're telling me this," Missy moans. "You want me to give Zach another chance. I just don't see how I can ever trust him again."

Ya-Ya pauses mixing the ingredients for her lemonade pie from memory; a dash of vanilla, fresh lemons, some sugar and cream, and begins to stir. Setting the spoon down, she looks Missy in the eye to make sure she hears her.

"In that moment, I knew he loved me and that he didn't care about any of those other girls. I didn't need to be jealous or feel insecure, because he only wanted to spend his life with me," she says. "A few weeks later, on one of our Sunday walks through town, he stopped at this very field," she says waving her spatula toward the window overlooking the back lawn and lake. She cocks her head, reliving the memory, and then says in a deep voice, mimicking Granddaddy, "I hope you don't mind, but I didn't get you a ring."

Missy chuckles at her grandmother's imitation of Granddaddy.

"I was confused," Ya-Ya continues, "and then he explained that he took his savings and bought this plot of land to build the Inn we had talked about. I didn't have a lot of plans, but I sure did have dreams, and your grandfather, he believed in me. We got married a few months later, right over there.

"Granddaddy's parents were furious, and told him we were on our own from there on out. I think they hoped that if they cut him off he would come to his senses and return to work at the bank, but we were determined to make our dreams come true. It was hard. People didn't come out to the lake back then like they do now. It was mostly just local fishing and swimming, but as word spread, more and more people started to visit."

Missy considers all the ingredients that made her grandparents relationship special and wonders if she and Zach's relationship share those same qualities.

"On our first anniversary I wanted to make something special to celebrate with Granddaddy, but our budget was stretched thin with starting the Inn. We were out of eggs, so I couldn't make his favorite lemon meringue pie, but I took the lemons and sugar we had and tried to make a version of lemon pie. It was a disaster, but Granddaddy gobbled it up and asked for seconds. I figured he was being kind to spare my feelings, but a few weeks later a young couple came in from the city to visit family in Pine Lake, and they asked me to make lemonade pie during their stay. I was confused by their request, but tried to remember each step I had taken with the last one, and

I guess it worked, because they ate the whole thing. Soon it was a regular request of guests staying at the Inn. Finally, Granddaddy told me he had sliced the rest of my lemonade pie and taken it over to the church for Bible study and choir practice. Everyone loved it, and soon, my pie was the talk of the town. There!" Ya-Ya says, using her spoon to make some decorative swirls in the top of the cream filling. "Now pop that into the fridge to set," she directed Missy.

"You make everything seem so easy," Missy says.

"It's just a choice," Ya-Ya says.

Missy sighs and licks the leftover pie off the mixing spoon.

"When someone works to make things right, you can choose to keep holding it against them, or you can choose to trust them. It's not that complicated," Ya-Ya says.

Missy collects the dirty mixing bowls and spoons and drops them into hot soapy water in the sink. Looking out the window she washes the dishes, turning Ya-Ya's story over in her mind.

She truly does make it seem so easy. How could she know she could trust Zach again?

Missy places the dishes in the drying rack and sinks into a chair at the table with Ya-Ya.

"I know you're scared," Ya-Ya says, taking Missy's hand in hers.

Missy's eyes well up with tears, thinking of all the people she's trusted and loved over the years, only to have them abandon her later on.

She and Emma's father had been dating for nearly two years, and they were in love—the forever kind of love, she thought. They had their whole future mapped out. She was going to be in international hotel management, and he was going into marketing, but things changed when she found out she was pregnant. She thought that they would move in together and she would stay in classes until Emma was born; after that, they would find a way to alternate their class schedules to care for Emma and study. She thought they were a team, but the minute he heard she was pregnant, he pulled away and she was left on her own. She went home to her parents for help and was met with more rejection. She feels lucky that Granddaddy and Ya-Ya had taken her in, and she has worked hard every day to make sure they never regretted their decision.

"Granddaddy and I were a team," Ya-Ya says. "He believed in me and helped my dreams come true, and I did the same for him, no matter how messy it got." Ya-Ya takes Missy's chin in her hands. "Are you understanding me?" She smiles.

"I think so." Missy nods.

Ya-Ya reaches into her apron pocket and hands Missy a handwritten note from Zach.

"He is special, that one." Ya-Ya says, beginning to wipe down the kitchen counters.

Missy unfolds the note and feels tears drip down her cheeks as she read Zach's words. Overwhelmed by the last few days, she folds the note and puts it into her pocket, wipes the tears from her face, and collects herself before greeting her guests for the day.

Chapter 16

The wheels of the plane touch down in Minneapolis as the light of the morning sun fills the cabin. Zach and Catherine wind their way through the busy airport filled with passengers looking for their gates and stopping for their morning coffee. They collect their bags and keys for the rental car and head outside, where they are met with the heavy humid summer air and the sound of taxis honking in the arrivals area.

Once settled into their rental car, they head toward the city. As they drive through the downtown area, Zach takes in the familiar skyline and points out local landmarks to Catherine. They exit onto Lake Harriet Parkway, a quiet two-lane road bordering the lake. Joggers, cyclists, and parents with strollers enjoy the summer day on the paved, tree-lined path in between the road and the lake. In this quieter suburb, they pull into the parking lot for a small redbrick office building with a big sign that reads "LWL Attorneys at Law."

They make their way upstairs and meet Scott in his office. After introductions and pleasantries, Scott brings Catherine up to speed, outlining the original charges from the United States Attorney's Office as well as the recent developments in their plea deal.

After their brief meeting, Scott shows Catherine to an office down the hall. She quickly gets settled and dives in to the boxes of discovery, poring over each document, trying to absorb every detail in order to piece together the financial puzzle that could clear Zach.

It's been nearly a week of twelve-hour days.

Rubbing her eyes, Catherine pulls out her phone. Scrolling through her notifications, she replies to her mom and Missy and a few friends. She opens her text thread with Blake, but there's been nothing new since before their fight at the picnic. Catherine was always the one to make the first move after a fight and she refused to be the one to call Blake this time, even though she couldn't stop thinking about him.

Putting her phone away, she turns her attention back to her computer and the box of discovery. She's exhausted, and even after several days, she still hasn't finished reviewing all the evidence in Zach's case. This isn't the first time, as a CPA, that she's been buried in paperwork, but it's more personal this time and she doesn't want to miss a thing. Catherine stares out the window, not really seeing the cars or people beyond the glass, wondering what she's missing—because things aren't adding up.

"Knock-knock," Scott calls as he pops his head into her office. "I come bearing gifts," he says, handing her a large iced mocha.

"If your plan is to keep me caffeinated until I solve the mystery, I'm not sure it's working," Catherine teases.

"The deal is only good until Friday, so something needs to come together in thirty-six hours," he says.

"Got it, so no pressure."

Catherine checks her phone again, but there's still no word from Blake.

Slamming it down, she returns her attention to the files on her desk, reading e-mails and footnotes on the audited financial statements, searching for any inconsistencies in the accounting.

"What's with you?" Scott asks.

"Just tired," Catherine smiles.

"Really? Because you're checking your phone nonstop, and I think your sweater's on backwards," Scott says.

"No it's not!" Catherine barks, looking down at the zipper on the front of her sweater.

"Is this a tag?" Scott says pointing to the collar of her sweater.

"Dammit. I thought this was a zip-front." Catherine sighs in frustration.

"It's okay. We're all tired," Scott says.

Just then, Scott's assistant Raquel pops her head in. "I'm sorry to interrupt, but Zach is on the line for you, Catherine."

Waving Scott out of her office, Catherine picks up the call.

"What's up?" she asks, then pauses to listen. "Sure, I'll meet you at Lake Harriet Park."

She grabs her iced coffee and phone and makes the short walk down the street, where she finds Zach waiting on a bench by the water.

"I don't understand why we couldn't just meet at the office," Catherine complains.

"Like I said, I just want to go over some things with you before showing them to Scott. I want to be sure," Zach says. He starts to tell Catherine about his meetings with Tracey, and shows her the information they uncovered about her dad's dealings.

As Catherine reviews the documents, the pieces of the accounting puzzle she has been working on all week finally start to fall into place. She is starting to see how these documents may explain the inconsistencies in the financials, and how Bill Anderson was able to manipulate investors in this deal.

They walk back to the office together, where Tracey joins them, and they call Scott, asking him to come to the conference room.

"What's going on?" Scott asks.

"When I got home from Pine Lake, I found this in my mail," Tracey says, handing Scott a bank statement for a company called TMA, Inc.

Tracey and Zach look at each other and then dive in, taking turns telling Catherine and Scott what they were able to discover in the past few days.

"I'm done burying my head in the sand," Tracey explains. "I need to know the truth of who my father is and what he did." She explains how she dug through all of her father's papers and files and opened the mail looking for any clue that might help Zach's case.

After opening the TMA statement, Tracey called the bank and learned she was the only signatory on the account, which had been opened over two years ago. She also learned that she had two more bank accounts under the names TMA2, Inc. and TMA3, Inc.

"With a little more digging, we found out they are owned by TMA Global, Inc., which is in the Cayman Islands," Tracey explains.

Catherine flips through the file of documents Tracey and Zach had brought, bank statements and incorporation papers. Opening her laptop, she opens a few spreadsheets and project them onto the large screen in the conference room.

"You're going to have to help me out. I'm a lawyer, not a CPA, remember?" Scott says, trying to make sense of the documents on the screen in front of him.

"This is the income statement, showing the last three years of income, expenses, and net profits."

"Okay, following you so far," Scott says.

"Look at the income in the column for 2016, and then for 2017. There's a 45 percent increase in revenue for both of those years, where for all the prior years it was at 3.5 percent."

"Are you trying to convince me that having a good year is a crime?" Scott asks.

"No, but falsifying your financials is," Catherine says. "In the discovery files you will find contracts with TMA which completely account for the increase in sales."

"Still not sure I am following," Scott says.

"That's okay, there's more," Catherine says, clicking open three more PDFs on her laptop. "The auditors sent out confirmations that the invoices for these sales would be paid, and each one was signed by none other than our friend, Mr. Anderson. And here are the financials for TMA. If you look right here, you will see they do not have the liability for the sale."

"So, the auditors made a mistake?" Scott asks.

"Not quite," Zach says, interrupting Catherine. "On the ride over here, I called a friend of mine who worked at Smith and Associates, handling Mr. Anderson's audit for years. Apparently she noticed the irregularity, but when she went to her boss about it, she was fired," Zach says.

Taking over Catherine's mouse, he clicks open a few more documents.

"What is this?" Scott asks.

"This is the e-mail where her boss threatened to fire her if she messed up this deal."

"Well, that isn't enough to prove Mr. Anderson manipulated all of this," Scott counters.

"Nope, but this might be," Catherine says, clicking open another file.

"What am I looking at?" Scott asks.

Catherine scrambles through the paper files spread out on the conference room table and looks up at the screen and breaks into a smile.

"What is it?" Zach asks.

Pointing to the projected document, she says, "Those are the wire transfers from TMA. They are the deposits on those new sales."

"So? We already knew that happened," Zach says.

"Right, but none of those bank statements were in discovery, so we didn't know that the money came from fictitious companies Mr. Anderson created in his daughter's name. He was just moving money around to fake sales, to make the numbers look good."

Scott is quiet, trying to digest everything Catherine and Zach had shared.

"Show this to the feds," Zach says. "Tell them I'm not their guy. I was manipulated and deceived by that greedy bastard!"

"I'm going to need you to explain this to the US Attorney," Scott says to Catherine.

Zach was anxious to get back to Pine Lake and talk to Missy and took the first flight back while Catherine spends the rest of the day compiling the additional bank statements and incorporation documents that Zach and Tracey found, along with the documents from the original discovery and her written report, summarizing Mr. Anderson's actions. Her report is clear and concise, and outlines with certainty that Mr. Anderson acted alone, and should bear full responsibility for the damages suffered by the investors.

After reviewing Catherine's report, Scott files a motion for summary judgment and submits it to the court.

With all the paperwork filed, Catherine heaves a sigh of relief, knowing they had done everything they could to help Zach resolve his case. She boards the plane back to Pine Lake and settles into the window seat.

Looking out the window as the plane lifts off, she smiles.

I've still got it, she thinks, proud of herself and the work she did on Zach's case. She hadn't worked much in the years since losing Aleksandra and she hadn't realized how much she had missed her work until this moment. She'd taken time away from work to rest and heal and had forgotten how good it feels to work through the challenges of a case, how much she loves being part of a top-notch team. Parts of her that she'd thought she had lost felt alive again.

Chapter 17

Scott had told Zach that it could take up to ninety days for the judge to rule on the motion. Zach knows he can't sit in Minnesota waiting for an answer without going crazy. He misses the sound of Missy's laughter and Emma's feet running through the Inn. He misses that feeling of warmth that he hadn't known before going to Pine Lake. He knows he messed things up horribly, but he has to go back.

Returning to Pine Lake in mid-June is far different from when he first arrived in late May. It is peak tourist season, and as he drives through town he sees that all the inns and motels have No Vacancy signs hung outside. The cottages dotting the shoreline have cars spilling out of their driveways. Even this early in the morning he can hear the low grumble of power boats racing down the lake. The coffee shop on Main Street has a line out the door, and their café tables out front are packed with families laughing and talking over their morning Danish.

He pulls into the parking lot of the Inn and drives up and down, looking for a spot, but they're all taken. He heads across the street to the overflow parking lot, where he finds someone pulling out of a spot in the back. At the crosswalk, he waits with families loaded down with beach bags and strollers and wagons with kids and coolers. The crowd smells of sunscreen.

When he reaches the Inn, he notices there's a bright yellow-and-white-striped awning over a large side window, proclaiming "Ya-Ya's Homemade Pies," with a long line of people stretching around the corner. The woman in front of him explains that the pie window opens at eight a.m. each day and closes when all the pies have sold out, so everyone lines up early to make sure they get one.

As he gets closer to the window, he can see Missy in a yellow golf shirt helping a team of employees in matching yellow golf shirts, some working the cash registers and others boxing up fresh pies. She has her curls pulled back from her face and is calling out orders to her staff, greeting her customers with her trademark friendly smile.

When it's finally Zach's turn, he approaches the window, excited to surprise Missy, but she barely looks up, busy talking to her staff.

A bit flustered, Zach realizes he doesn't know what to say. He finally clears his throat and mumbles, "So you're selling Ya-Ya's pies now?"

Missy looks startled to see him. "You're back?" she asks.

"I was hoping we could talk for a few minutes," Zach says.

Missy looks at the crowd waiting behind Zach and at the busyness in her kitchen, just as one of her staff announces that they only have a dozen pies left.

Zach checks his watch. It's 8:45, and the line is still snaking through the parking lot.

"Is every day this busy?" he asks.

"This really isn't a good time, Zach."

Zach nods. "Yeah, I guess not. I'll just take a pie then."

Transaction completed, Zach fiddles with his keys, watching as Missy continues to greet each customer with her friendly smile and easy laugh.

Suddenly, he sees Ya-Ya at his side.

"She isn't busy at sunrise," Ya-Ya says with a wink, handing him a notepad and pen.

Zach accepts the pen and paper, scribbles out a note, and hands everything back to Ya-Ya.

She gives him a gentle squeeze and then heads inside, presumably to deliver his note.

Zach takes in the lively crowd around him. He can't help but smile, knowing how much this boom in business must mean to Missy and her family.

He starts to head to his car when he hears his name. He turns back and sees Missy waving and jogging his way.

He waves back and smiles at her.

"So, I'll see you tomorrow?" Missy asks when she reaches him.

Zach nods, speechless that she agreed. Finally finding his words he adds, "The pie window looks great."

"You may have been right about selling Ya-Ya's pie," she says with a laugh.

"I know a thing or two about business."

"Well, I have to get back," she says, and returns to the Inn.

Back in his car, Zach rests his head on the steering wheel, replaying his words.

I know a thing or two about business. Who says that?

Zach drives back to his dad's house and parks his car in the driveway. A month ago, when he'd first returned to his dad's, it was late and dark and barely summer. Now summer is in full swing, the grass is lush and green, and the mountain laurel surrounding the house is waving its fuchsia flowers.

In May, Zach had dreaded coming to Pine Lake, but now, just four weeks later, so much has changed. He doesn't want to waste any more of his life holding a grudge against his dad. Sure, he wasn't the best father, but he did his best. It's just who he is.

His dad is on the riding mower in the side yard, and Zach offers a wave before heading inside. Once in the kitchen, he drops his bags and sets the pie on the island, pouring two glasses of iced tea from the pitcher that was on the counter.

Blake comes in a few moments later.

"When did you get back?" Blake asks, washing up at the kitchen sink.

"I landed early this morning."

"Been by to see Missy?" Blake asks, pointing at the pie.

"I tried to," Zach says, cutting them each a slice and joining his dad at the kitchen table.

Zach feels his phone buzzing in his pocket. When he takes it out he sees a notification from Scott with a YouTube link to a breaking news story on CNN. Zach moves his chair next to Blake's and turns the phone towards him so they can both watch the YouTube video.

They listen to the reporter standing outside the Minneapolis police station as he announces that Mr. Bill Anderson of North American Foods was taken into custody just hours before. The station flips to footage of officers escorting a handcuffed man from a black SUV into the police station.

"Is this your case?" Blake asks.

Zach raises a hand to shush his dad as he listens to the reporter state that the US Attorney has charged Mr. Anderson with conspiracy to commit fraud, among many other charges.

After the video finishes, Zach calls Scott.

"They are dropping all charges against you in exchange for your testimony against Mr. Anderson," Scott explains.

"It's over," Zach says in disbelief.

Zach exhaled with relief. For the last few months all he could think about was how his life was over and now he had another chance, thanks to Scott and Catherine and Tracey's help at unwinding Mr. Anderson's crimes.

"That's good news," Blake says.

Zach nods, shaking his head. He's speechless.

Blake takes another bite of pie and asks, "Does this mean you fixed things with Missy, too?"

Some things never change, Zach thinks, but instead, says, "I'm working on it."

After cleaning up the dishes, Zach heads upstairs to his room. He collapses on his bed, exhausted from his early flight, but more so, the stress of the past few months.

He pulls Emma's stick figure drawing out of his wallet. He carefully unfolds it and traces the images she drew of the three of them holding hands, with the lake in the background. He sets it on his nightstand and drifts off to sleep, thinking about Missy.

Chapter 18

After getting in from Minnesota, Catherine crawls into bed and turns on the television to an old romantic comedy she knew all the words to, and quickly falls asleep.

Waking up a few hours later, she feels more rested than she had anticipated. She thinks about how much of her life she's planned around Blake during their relationship. She moved to Pine Lake for him. Sold her house in the city for him. She hadn't realized until her trip to Minnesota how much she'd put her life on pause for him. This trip had been a wake-up call. It was time for her to get back to living her life.

She climbs out of bed and heads to the bathroom. Her face in the mirror looks red and puffy; her eyes are swollen, and her cheeks are streaked with mascara. She pulls her hair up into a messy bun and splashes some cold water on her face, puts on an old pair of jeans and a T-shirt. Seeing Blake's hoodie lying over the chair in her bedroom, she grabs it and stuffs it into the bottom drawer of her dresser. *Out of sight, out of mind.*

Downstairs in the kitchen, she turns on the kettle to make herself a cup of hot tea and opens the sliding door to feel to cool morning breeze. On the nearby end table, she sees the picture of her and Blake, ice-skating, shortly after they met. It had always been one of her favorites, but now when she looks at it, she feels sad and angry. She scoops it up, along with other photos of them in the living room, and dumps them into an empty box in the garage. She takes another look around the living room to make sure there are no more reminders of him.

That's better, she thinks, as she hears the kettle whistle.

She pours her tea into a travel mug, grabs some carrots for the horses, and heads outside to the wooded trail near her home. She is lost in her thoughts as her feet lead the way along the soft bed of fallen pine needles, each step releasing the woodsy scent. She stops at a creek that intersects the path and kicks a rock along its edge. She climbs up onto a boulder bordering the edge of the creek and pulls her knees tight into her chest and listens to the water bubbling as it moves downstream.

Closing her eyes, she feels the tears burn as they slide down her cheeks.

Why am I so hard for him to love?

She thinks back on the fights they have had, where she has begged and pleaded for a romantic weekend away on their anniversary, or a special night for her birthday, but he couldn't make the time.

He has time for work, for any neighbor that asks for something from him, so why not me?

"Why can't you love me?" she cries out, disrupting the quiet of the woods.

She climbs off the boulder and picks up a handful of small rocks. Throwing one into the water, she shouts, "What did I do wrong?" Then another. "Why don't you miss me?" And a third. "Why didn't you call me?" With each thought, she shouts louder and throws the rocks harder, until she is overcome with tears and slumps down onto the bed of pine needles.

She listens to the sound of the creek gurgling past her until her tears slow to a trickle. Hearing the birds sing in the canopy overhead, she wipes the tears from her cheeks and begins to feel her body relax. She watches two squirrels run past her and chase each other around the trunk of a tree. Feeling calmer, she brushes the pine needles from her jeans and starts to walk back down the trail toward home. As the trail ends, the trees thin and she sees the barn and hears the whinny of her horses.

She heads over to the barn to visit Breezy and Tinka.

"Good afternoon. I brought you treats," she says, opening the stall door and offering Breezy a carrot. She nuzzles her face into the warmth of the horse's neck. "I missed you," she says.

She grabs the pitchfork and wheelbarrow and starts mucking out the stall. She scoops the dirty bedding into the wheelbarrow and when it's full, she takes it to the back side of the barn and dumps it, repeating the process until the stall is completely clean. She nuzzles Breezy again before tossing down new bedding, giving her clean water, and filling the hay holder with fresh hay.

Moving to the next stall, she greets Tinka, gives her a carrot, and repeats the process. Of course, her stable hand would be in to clean and care for the horses like he did every other day, but after the mental and emotional challenge of the last few weeks, it felt good to move her body and work up a sweat.

Taking a break, she checks her phone and sees a message from Zach with the news that the charges against him had been dropped.

She quickly texts him back a note of congratulations and breaks out into a silly dance, yelling "We did it! We did it!"

She leaves the barn and races across the yard and down to the dock. Tossing her phone to the ground and stripping off her jeans and T-shirt, she runs down the dock and does a cannonball into the lake. Shrieking with delight, she hits the water with a splash. The water is cool and refreshing, and she can't stop smiling as she floats around on her back. Closing her eyes, she feels the sun on her face and tries to savor the moment.

When she begins to feel the chill of the water, she swims over to the dock and climbs out. Finding an Adirondack chair in a sunny spot, she sits and enjoys the stillness of the lake.

She feels like it's the first time in years she has actually been still. Her mind goes back to last year's Fourth of July weekend. Her nieces had come for a visit, and they were so excited they were up before daybreak, hopping on her bed, asking for pancakes.

Bleary-eyed, she'd gotten out of bed and made pancakes with them. They'd eaten on the deck, enjoying the early-morning breeze. After their breakfast they had changed into their swimsuits, slathered on the sunscreen, and raced down to the dock, excited to go tubing. Catherine smiles, remembering the laughter and silliness they'd shared on the lake, and how disappointed she was that Blake hadn't joined them—how many other moments she was alone because Blake was too busy working. He missed holidays, birthdays, anniversaries, and all of the small, everyday moments, like an afternoon on the lake.

She longed to share all her moments with Blake, so for the past year she had tried orchestrating special events, each one failing more brilliantly than the last. After what had happened at the Slice of Summer Picnic and his lack of contact while she was in Minneapolis with Zach, she knew she couldn't fight any longer. She was heartbroken, and exhausted.

Her reverie is interrupted by Blake's voice, calling to her. It was just like Blake to act like everything was normal; to sweep their conflict under the rug. She felt her body stiffen and her walls go up

"You heard about Zach?"

"I just heard," Catherine calls back.

Blake sits down next to her. "From Lakeside Bakery," he says, handing her her favorite iced coffee and a pumpkin muffin.

"Thank you."

She says nothing else, staring out across the lake. She had a long history with Blake and after he didn't reach out to her after their most recent fight she felt resigned to the fact that their relationship didn't work.

"I was hoping we could talk," Blake says, breaking their silence. "I was surprised I didn't hear from you while you were in Minnesota."

Catherine continues staring out over the lake, considering his words before speaking. "After how you yelled at me at the picnic, I thought you might be the one to reach out first, to apologize," she says.

"You're right. I should have called you," he says. "I definitely over-reacted. And you were right about things with me and Zach. You're just better at this than me."

"I know," Catherine says. "I was always good at being a mom, and I could tell Zach needed that."

"Aleksandra was lucky to have you."

"I was lucky to have her, and you're lucky to have Zach. He loves you," Catherine says.

"What about you?" Blake asks.

"What about me?" Catherine asks.

"Do *you* love me?" Blake asks.

Catherine sets down her coffee and gazes out over the lake. "You know I do," she begins.

"I can feel a *but* coming," Blake interrupts.

153

"But . . . I feel like we need different things. It feels like our lives are heading in different directions," she offers.

"So, you just want to throw away what we have?"

"Maybe. I don't know."

"What's done is done. Can we just start over?" Blake asks. "I'm doing my best here. I'm giving you everything I have."

Catherine turns toward Blake and puts her hand on his. "I know you are."

"I can't believe this," Blake says, standing up and shoving his hands in his pockets. "How can you just walk away?"

"I just feel like we'd make each other miserable if we stay together, and then we'll resent each other, and I don't want that," she says, standing up.

Blake stares at his feet. "So what are you saying?"

"I think we need a break," she says.

Blake fiddles with his baseball cap in silence for a moment, then walks off.

"Good-bye, Blake," Catherine whispers to herself, listening to the crunch of his tires pulling out of her driveway.

Sinking back into her chair, she pulls her knees into her chest. Watching a pair of dragonflies dancing on the edge of the dock, she realizes she's feeling a calm she hasn't felt in years.

Chapter 19

It's early, and nearly all the guests are still asleep, so Missy shuts her bedroom door and quietly finds her way down the hall.

In the great room, she checks her watch. It's 5:30 a.m., still a half-hour to go until sunrise.

Over on the sofa, she sees a woman curled up by the fire, reading a book. At the coffee station, there is a man who looks far too alert for this time of morning, filling his thermos and ready to start his day. She smiles and whispers good morning to these guests before making herself a cup of coffee and heading outside to the back deck.

Summer mornings in the mountains are chilly, so she wraps a blanket around herself and settles into a rocker to wait for Zach. Resting her feet on the deck railing she takes a deep breath and sinks deeper into her chair. It is still fairly dark, but the sunlight is starting to peek out from behind the mountains, enough so she can make out a thick layer of fog on the lake.

Missy blows on her hot coffee and thinks back to her conversation with Zach after the picnic—how she'd met Tracey, and learned about the gravity of his legal issues.

It's almost like she could get over the Tracey thing. Sure, she'd felt insecure and jealous—Tracey was drop-dead gorgeous, after all—but knowing that Zach had hidden the truth about his legal issues, well, that made her feel like he couldn't trust her with all that he was facing. That was what had hurt the most. After Ya-Ya's talk with her, however, she is feeling less angry and less hurt. There is definitely something between them. And that is worth saving.

Hearing the door open, Missy turns to see Zach.

"Over here," she calls from the far end of the deck.

Zach heads toward her, unsure of how she will react to a hug or a kiss, but when he leans in, she wraps her arms around him and doesn't turn her cheek when he kisses her good morning.

"Let's sit on the dock. It has the best views for a sunrise," she suggests.

"What's all of this?" she asks, noticing he's carrying a basket.

"Ya-Ya," he says, smiling.

"I see. I think you've made quite an impression on her."

"She's something else, isn't she?"

As they cross the back lawn to the dock, Zach reaches for Missy's hand. She slides her fingers between his and gives his hand a squeeze.

For a while they sit on the dock, just drinking their coffee in silence.

Zach folds and unfolds his napkin into triangles while trying to figure out where to start.

"Mmm, this is so good," Zach says, taking a bite of the blueberry muffin Ya-Ya baked for them.

"I know." Missy laughs.

"You really do have the best laugh. I've missed it," Zach says.

She smiles in response.

156

Zach remains silent while they watch the sky turn from shades of orange to pink as the sun begins to rise above the mountain, reflecting like a glowing orb on the smooth surface of the lake.

"So, you must be thrilled that the charges have been dropped," Missy says.

"Absolutely!" Zach says. "Catherine was a lifesaver."

He explains the work she did and the additional evidence they compiled and submitted to the US Attorney.

"My lawyer says there is no way the charges would have been dropped without her work."

"I'm so happy for you," Missy offers.

"I didn't tell you because I didn't' want to make this morning all about me and my lawsuit," Zach clarifies.

Missy looks at Zach and then turns her gaze out to the lake, praying it will lessen the awkwardness between them. She wants to bury herself in his arms and tell him how happy she is that his legal issues are resolved, how much she's missed him and how glad she is that he came back, but she can't sweep the secrets and lies under the rug and ignore them.

"I'm trying to think of the right words to say, to explain things," Zach starts. "But I can't. I don't know how to fix this."

Missy wants to comfort him, but she can't. It's not okay that he didn't tell her about Tracey, or the extent of his legal troubles. She needs an explanation. She needs to understand if any of what they've shared is real.

"I messed up," Zach says.

Missy feels a tightness in her chest, remembering Tracey at the Slice of Summer Picnic and how she hung on Zach. *Tall and thin and beautiful, completely perfect*, she thinks, looking down at herself in her old leggings and hoodie.

"You lied to me," Missy says.

Zach nods. "I did. And I wish I hadn't. I'm so sorry that I wasn't honest with you."

Looking out over the lake, Zach tells her the whole story.

When he's finished, he takes a deep breath, trying to shake off the anger and frustration he feels, being forced to recount all that he'd endured the past few months.

Missy dips her toes into the lake and watches the ripples, processing all that Zach had shared.

"So why did you come here, really?" she asks.

"I couldn't leave my house without being mobbed by reporters. They were camped out on my mother's front lawn, so I couldn't go there either. Coming here felt like my only option."

Missy studies Zach's face, trying to compare it to the first time she saw him, when he'd come into the Inn and his card was declined. She remembers him looking weary. She remembers how over their time together, he relaxed, and his smile seemed to come a little bit easier. In his weeks at Pine Lake his skin had quickly tanned, and a spark had returned to his eyes.

"The whole thing felt so unfair. I didn't do the deal on my own, but I was the only one being charged. I was carrying all the responsibility," he explains.

While Missy has compassion for the stress caused by the case, that certainly doesn't cover not telling her he had a girlfriend, and she feels the heat rise to her cheeks, thinking about it.

"What about Tracey?" she blurts out.

"I should have told you about her. I know it sounds pathetic, but it was complicated."

Missy sighs. The sun is higher in the sky and the air is warming; she peels off her hoodie and enjoys feeling the sun's warmth on her shoulders.

Zach explains that he'd first met Tracey because she was Mr. Anderson's daughter, and soon, they found themselves traveling in the same social circles. Their relationship wasn't love at first sight, but more a relationship birthed out of circumstance, of people moving along the same path in life who enjoyed spending time together. They grew to care for each other, but maybe it was more a friendship than a romance.

Then Mr. Anderson had disappeared, and it divided them. Tracey was dealing with her grief over her dad leaving and trying to emotionally support her mom, and all of Zach's energy was focused on dealing with his criminal charges. They hadn't seen or talked to one another in months.

"Our priorities changed, and our relationship sort of withered."

Zach looks depleted.

Missy picks at her fingernail polish, thinking about all he has said.

"I meant what I said in my note," he continues. "I know I hurt you, and I will do whatever it takes to fix things between us," Zach says, gazing into her eyes.

Missy meets his gaze but doesn't reply.

"When I met you, I wasn't ready to look at what a mess I'd made out of my life, much less share any of it," he says.

Missy gets tears in her eyes and sniffs to hold them back.

Zach moves closer to Missy, wrapping his arms around her, and she lets her head rest on his shoulder.

Trust has been tricky for her ever since her relationship with her parents disintegrated. She had just assumed they would be there for her and support her, no matter what, because they loved her, but that's not what happened. Instead, they had shut her out because they disagreed with her life choices.

When she fell in love with Emma's dad, she had thought they were a team. While they hadn't exactly made plans for a future together, they certainly had talked about things, and she thought they both envisioned a shared future. But she had been mistaken about that, too, and he had slipped out of her life, and out of Emma's.

She is grateful that Zach has shared all of this with her; he has been really open with her. Honestly, she doesn't know how she would have acted if she were in his shoes.

But a voice inside her still asks, What if she is wrong about him, too?

"I love you," Zach whispers into her ear.

Missy closes her eyes, wraps her arms around him, and tries to enjoy this moment, and not overthink it.

Ya-Ya tells Missy she will take care of Emma so she and Zach can spend the rest of the day together, which they do. They act like typical tourists, swimming in the lake, napping on the beach, talking over a lazy lunch, during which Zach mentions he has a friend in the city who could help her distribute and sell her pies across the country.

After saying good-bye to Zach, Missy sits on the deck, replaying their day over in her mind. He was so open with her, and seemed to be sorry. They had had a wonderful time together.

When it came to his ideas about expanding her business, however, it felt a bit overwhelming. She'd been completely surprised at his suggestion that she mass-produce Ya-Ya's pies and sell them all across the country, but his offer to arrange a meeting with his business associate in distribution was generous. She had so much to consider. Ya-Ya's pies were special because she oversaw each one being made, and sent them out full of her love. Her pies were meant to be a blessing to those who ate them, not simply one of the items you toss into your cart at the supermarket.

Not to mention, how could she juggle one more thing? Between caring for Emma and Ya-Ya and the Inn, she was already flat out.

She found herself playing a game of What if. What if it didn't work? What if she couldn't handle it? What if people didn't like the pies and she lost everything and her family ended up homeless? It felt too risky.

Missy hears the sliding door open and Ya-Ya steps out onto the deck. "Come with me," Ya-Ya says.

Descending the steps from the deck, they walk across the back lawn to the gazebo in the lavender garden. Ya-Ya sits down on the bench and pats the seat next to her, inviting Missy to join her. They sit in silence for a few moments and Missy watches the butterflies dance across the lavender surrounding the gazebo before she tearfully spills every detail of her conversation with Zach.

Ya-Ya listens and waits for Missy to catch her breath. She points to the edge of the garden and says, "Granddaddy bought me my first lavender plant when we opened the Inn. Every spring I divided them, and now look!"

"You have a beautiful garden," Missy offers with a sniffle.

"*We* have a beautiful garden," Ya-Ya corrects her, taking Missy's hand in hers.

Missy runs her fingers across Ya-Ya's leathery hand, feeling the deep wrinkles time has left.

"This garden started before that first plant. It started with my dream. Granddaddy believed in me, and over the years, one plant at a time, we built this garden. We built the Inn, and now, my legacy to you—a pie empire," Ya-Ya says with a giggle.

"But you had Granddaddy. I'm in this all alone," Missy says.

"I think you're only in this alone if you choose to be."

"I don't know if I can do it," Missy admits.

"When I made that first pie to shower Granddaddy with love, I never imagined it could turn into any of this. Look around you. What if Zach's idea is the start of *your* garden?"

Missy stares off past the garden and the back lawn to the shore of the lake. She watches as the water gently laps at the sand. She sees a little girl squeal and run back to her parents' beach blanket as the water tickles her ankles.

Missy smiles and thinks back to when her life was that simple. All it took was a day by the water with her parents for life to be perfect. Now she has Emma and Ya-Ya and the Inn to worry about.

"I have to go make my rounds," Ya-Ya says.

She pats Missy's knee and heads back toward the Inn.

Ya-Ya and Granddaddy's relationship had always felt magical to Missy: the way Granddaddy left Ya-Ya little love notes on the fridge, telling her he loved her; or how Ya-Ya would watch Granddaddy work in the garden in the late summer heat and greet him on the back deck with a pitcher of iced tea; how they'd sit on their rocking chairs in the shade, talking for hours.

Missy longed for a fairy tale like theirs. What if Zach was the respectful and loving partner her heart had been wishing for?

She wanders through the lavender garden, looking at all the plants, and stops at one. She bends down and picks a sprig of the lavender and gently rolls it between her thumb and forefinger, releasing its oils. She inhales the calming fragrance and looks out over the garden and the back lawn and then back to the Inn, looking fresh from its recent renovations, and smiles.

She knows she is ready for whatever comes next.

Chapter 20

Catherine sits up in bed and looks around her room. The floor is covered in days' worth of discarded clothing. Her suitcase still sits where she dropped it after coming home from Minnesota, and a pizza box balances precariously on her nightstand.

She has spent most of her days since her conversation with Blake wearing ratty sweatpants, lying in bed, or crying on the couch, watching sappy romance movies and eating pizza straight from the box.

Even though deep down she's excited for Missy and her meeting with the distributor, she hasn't had her normal energy. She doesn't feel like she's being a very supportive friend.

She forces herself to climb in the shower and put on fresh clothes, but draws the line at washing and blowing out her hair. A messy bun would have to do for today. After dabbing on some concealer and mascara, she checks her reflection in the mirror; not horrid, she thinks.

She scoops up the piles of dirty laundry and dumps them into a basket, then makes her bed before heading downstairs. In the living room she collects more empty pizza boxes, empty water bottles, discarded coffee mugs, and her notebooks and pens. She straightens up her throw blankets and opens the curtains to let some sunlight in.

Much better.

Catherine makes a fresh pitcher of iced tea and mixes together some chicken salad for her lunch date with Missy. She opens the door to the back deck and waves to a neighbor who's fishing down by the shore, then opens the umbrella over the patio table.

She hears Missy calling hello as she lets herself in the front door.

Catherine goes inside to greet her with a warm hug.

"I've missed you," Catherine says, hugging Missy tightly.

In the kitchen, Catherine pours them each a glass of iced tea and they head outside to catch up.

"Tell me everything I missed while I was away," Catherine says.

Missy fills Catherine in on the final renovations at the Inn, their flourishing reservations and glowing reviews, her new pie window, and the presentation about mass-producing pies, scheduled for the next day.

"I'm so happy for you," Catherine says warmly. "You have worked so hard—you deserve all of this success!"

"Thank you," Missy says, eyes glistening.

"Come with me—I have something for you," Catherine says, taking Missy by the hand.

In Catherine's bedroom, Missy plops down on the edge of Catherine's bed like a teenager at a sleepover.

Catherine heads into her closet and calls out, "Are you ready?" before presenting Missy with a black skirt suit and ice-blue blouse.

Missy's mouth drops open. "For me?"

Catherine nods.

Ripping everything off the hangers, Missy on the outfit, turning from side to side in front of Catherine's full-length mirror, trying to take in how professional she looks.

"You're going to kill it at your meeting tomorrow," Catherine reassures her.

"I'm scared," she says. "What if I allow myself to feel excited and then I end up losing it all? Maybe if I don't get excited at all, it won't matter when it doesn't work out."

"Ahhh, the old hope for the best, expect the worst scenario," Catherine says.

"Just feels like it would make things easier."

"Not enjoying the excitement won't make disappointment any less painful—living that way just means you miss out on all the happiness and joy in life," Catherine offers.

"This guy runs a real business with locations all over the country, and then there's me—a small-town girl whose grandmother makes pies. What if I make a fool of myself?" Missy asks.

"You're not giving yourself enough credit. This guy agreed to a meeting because he is interested in you, and what you have to offer. You can do this!"

"What if he only agreed to meet with me as a favor to Zach," Missy says.

Catherine wraps her arms around Missy, smoothing her hair. She had always imagined sharing moments like this with Aleksandra. When she'd lost her, she assumed she had also lost out on these kind of moments, too. She offers silent gratitude; she's so lucky to have Missy in her life.

"Thank you so much for the suit," Missy says.

Catherine smiles and goes into her closet, pulling a box down from the shelf.

"The right shoes are what really make an outfit, and these have never let me down. I closed every deal when I wore these shoes," Catherine says, handing the box to Missy.

Missy opens the box and eyes a pair of gorgeous black stilettos. She's not sure how she'll be able to walk in them, but hurriedly slides them on her feet. She hobbles over to Catherine's full-length mirror, twirling around in her power suit and heels. She breaks out into a little happy dance, trying not to roll an ankle. Catherine and Missy collapse into a fit of giggles.

But Missy's excitement disappears as quickly as it had bubbled up. "I don't know," Missy says, sitting down on the bed. "I just feel like everything I touch, I ruin."

"Why would you think that?" Catherine asks, joining her on the bed.

"I mean, I got pregnant and had to drop out of college. I have had to rely on my grandparents to take care of me and employ me. I haven't been able to keep a boyfriend for long. I just can't do anything right," Missy says.

"That's not how I see things. Look at you. You finished college while raising Emma. That takes a lot of dedication. You could have given up, but you finished because it was important to you."

"Maybe, but it's only because I had Ya-Ya and Granddaddy's help."

"You don't have to do things on your own for them to count," Catherine says. "You know that, right?"

"Yeah. I guess you're right. Thanks for always knowing what to say. And for all of your support." Missy looks closely at Catherine. "Now spill—how have things been with Blake?"

Catherine leans back against the pillows of her king-size bed, thinking about the past few days. She rolls on her side to face Missy. "I ended things with Blake."

"What? When?"

"When I got back from Minneapolis." Catherine says, and suddenly starts to cry.

Missy grabs a tissue from the nightstand and gently dabs Catherine's tears, pulling her into a hug.

"Are you okay?" she asks.

"Yeah. I think so. It all feels so complicated." Catherine pauses, takes a breath. "It felt so good, working on Zach's case. I felt alive in a way I haven't felt in a long time. But Blake didn't call or text the whole time I was gone,"

"Wow, I'm sorry. Is it really over between you two?" Missy asks

"Yes. I think being away helped me realize more about who Blake really is. And that's not what I want," Catherine says.

Missy takes Catherine's hand in hers and listens as Catherine explains how many times she has tried talking to Blake and sharing her feeling, but that nothing ever changed.

"I feel like I can finally see the truth of our relationship. I love him so much, but I can't keep wishing and hoping and waiting for things to be different."

"Blake is like family to me, and I love you both dearly, but he doesn't always make his relationships a priority," Missy offers.

"I think the most painful kind of loneliness is when you feel alone when you're with someone you love," Catherine says.

"I'm so sorry," Missy says hugging her tightly.

Catherine brushes away her tears. "I don't want to be a downer and rain on your parade. You have your big meeting and your Fourth of July picnic coming up. Let's focus on those things!"

"It's okay for you to be sad. I know you're happy for me, but don't forget—I'm here for you, too," Missy reassures her.

Catherine nods and they head downstairs for lunch. They make their way out to the deck to enjoy their chicken salad sandwiches and iced tea. Catherine feels her stress dissolve as they quickly fall into their usual banter. Soon they are laughing like until they can't catch their breath, or even remember what was so funny.

Catherine smiles at Missy, so grateful to have a friend who gets her—who can take her from a sobbing mess over a man to laughing until her face hurts.

Chapter 21

Missy throws her hair up into a loose ponytail picks up her notes. Pencil between her teeth, she paces back and forth in the Inn's conference room, reviewing her notes on co-packing costs, recipe modifications for commercial sale, cost per unit, and marketing plan. She furiously scrawls notes on her lined yellow pad and then resumes her pacing, until she reaches the end of her presentation.

You're ready. Time to call it a night, she thinks, turning off the lights and closing the conference room door.

She knows she should head directly to bed and get a good night's sleep, but her brain is too worked up, and won't quiet down. Rather than going to her quarters, she grabs a sweatshirt from her office and makes her way down the quiet hallway to the back deck and across the lawn. She plops down on the dock, pulls her sweatshirt tighter across her chest, and dangles her toes in the warm water of the lake.

Exhaling deeply, she looks up at the full moon, begging it for all the answers she wants.

Why can't she just relax and enjoy things with Zach, and see where they go?

Closing her eyes, she rubs a finger over her thumb, imagining it's Zach, tracing his thumb over hers. She can feel it tingle, and her stomach flip-flops just like it did when she was with him that morning.

She feels her shoulders relax as the tension flows out of her body. When she is with Zach, she feels like she can breathe again. She fears she's being a silly, starry-eyed girl, missing all the red flags, but she can't help it. Somehow, things feel so right and easy with him.

She thinks back to the first day she met him, when he'd stumbled into the Inn looking for a room. His clothes and shoulders screamed tense and uptight, but his eyes told a different story; they were soft and tender, and told her there was more to him than his tough exterior.

That first night when they'd had dinner and talked, he was vulnerable and honest, and playful and gentle as they swam under the stars. Watching him with Emma, she could tell he was kind. He was a natural with her, teaching her to fish and hoisting her up on his shoulders.

She closes her eyes and sees herself in her mind's eye, moving like an old-time movie.

It's her presentation the next day. She's always been able to see herself dressed in a business suit with a briefcase in her hand, but her movie is different this time. Zach is there, at the end of the hallway. He's laughing and saying something. She can't hear the words, but she smiles and laughs. He's holding the door for her, and his eyes—the way they look at her—she can tell he adores her.

Zach gestures for her to go in, and he follows right behind. She is standing at the front of the room. Zach takes a seat at the conference table, turning his chair toward her, giving her his full attention. She begins her presentation. He nods along as she is talking. She has a clicker in her hand and is advancing slides on a large screen behind her. She doesn't have notes or stand at a podium. Instead, she is talking freely and advancing her slides, like she has shared this information thousands of times. She fields questions from the small group of men and women in suits. She laughs and they laugh, though again, she can't hear the words. It's clear she is engaging, and they are interested in her presentation. In her movie, she feels confident and calm. She feels alive.

This portion of the movie ends, and she feels Zach's hand slide into hers as they slowly leave the room, hand in hand.

Taking one last look at the moon, she silently thanks it for the answers she needed and heads back inside. Climbing into bed, she picks up her phone and sends Zach a text before turning off her bedside lamp and letting sleep wash over her.

Missy pours herself a cup of coffee and takes time getting ready in her black suit and heels. Tucking her curls behind her ears, she takes one last look in the mirror before heading to the conference room to make sure everything is set up for her presentation. She hooks her laptop up to the projector and tests all the settings, making sure her slide deck loads. Off to the side, she sets her packaging mock-ups with the new logo on a stand.

She takes in how the conference room looks, arranging the coffee and tea on the side table, so everything is perfect. She checks her watch: five minutes until her presentation.

Zach comes into the room. "Everything looks great!" he says.

"Then why do I feel like a little kid playing dress-up?" she asks.

Missy's staff knocks on the conference room door. "Missy, your ten o'clock meeting is here."

"Thanks, . Please send him in."

Turning to Zach, Missy offers him a quick thank you for arranging this meeting and straightens her jacket before turning towards the doorway to greet Joseph Jackson.

Joseph Jackson is a tall man in his early fifties with broad shoulders and salt-and-pepper hair. He is tanned and dressed casually in chinos and a button-down shirt, with the sleeves rolled up.

"Good morning, Mr. Jackson. Thank you for taking the time to meet with me today," Missy says, smiling and extending her hand.

"Please, call me Joseph," he says warmly. "Zach has told me so many great things about you and your business. I'm intrigued."

Missy offers him coffee and a tour of their operations. As she walks Joseph through the Inn, she shares with him her grandmother's dream to start this Inn, and how an anniversary surprise evolved into a sign of love and kindness among the community here in Pine Lake.

As they approach the kitchen, she tells Joseph how they have moved from preparing individual pies to making larger batches and selling them through the pie window. While he enjoys a sample of Ya-Ya's lemonade pie, she emphasizes their commitment to fresh and local ingredients.

Back in the conference room, she dims the lights and starts the projector, walking him through the detailed costs of co-packing and distribution, packaging samples, and marketing plans.

Joseph listens with rapt attention, taking notes as she talks and asking questions throughout her presentation.

Zach sits quietly at the conference table. Watching her ace her presentation leaves him feeling as alive as if it were his deal.

After Missy concludes her presentation and answers Joseph's final questions, she thanks him for coming and walks him out.

When Missy returns to the conference room, Zach scoops Missy up and twirls her around. "Your presentation was flawless. He was hanging on every word. You nailed it!"

Missy smiles from ear to ear.

"Thank you," she says, feeling grateful not just for Zach's feedback, but also for his belief in her, and support of her dreams. In fact, he'd been so confident in her abilities that he'd put his name and reputation on the line by coordinating her pitch meeting with Mr. Jackson.

"I have a surprise for you," Zach says.

Missy looks at him quizzically.

"Meet me down at the dock," Zach says.

Back in her room, Missy squeals and dances around, feeling the rush of excitement from her successful presentation. She changes into her bikini, throws a sundress over that, grabs her beach bag, and practically skips down to the dock.

She pauses on the back lawn for a moment to watch Zach.

He has carefully rolled up the sleeves of his button-down, and she can see the muscles of his forearms flexing as he pulls back the boat cover and stores it away. In his swim trunks and boat shoes, she can see that his legs are golden, and his light brown hair has turned sandy blond from the sun. His shoulders seem more relaxed.

Zach's face lights up when he sees her, and she runs the rest of the way. On the dock she drops her bag and jumps into his arms, wrapping her legs around his waist. She feels Zach's arms holding her tight.

"Your carriage awaits," Zach teases, setting Missy down in the boat.

Pushing away from the dock, Zach slowly motors them down the lake.

Missy closes her eyes, feeling the cool breeze blow through her hair. Zach reaches over for her hand and her fingers slide easily between his.

They approach a small cove, where Zach slows the boat and sets anchor at a nearby sandy island. Zach leads Missy ashore to a picnic carefully arranged on the beach. She sits down on the blanket and

Zach pulls a chilled bottle of wine from the cooler and pours them each a glass.

"You thought of everything," Missy says, accepting her glass.

"I knew you were going to be terrific," Zach says, giving her a kiss.

"My cheeks hurt from smiling so much today." Missy laughs.

"I mean it, you really did great today," Zach says.

"It felt good," Missy says, leaning her head on Zach's chest.

"I'll be honest—I wasn't sure how it was going to feel to watch from the sidelines, but it was amazing."

Missy blushes.

"When I'm with you, I feel inspired again," he says. "I want to support you in all your dreams—in everything you do in life."

When she'd gotten pregnant with Emma, nearly everyone in her life had told her she would never see any of her dreams come true, but that had changed when she met Zach. *That's because he sees opportunity where others see obstacles*, she realizes. He believes in her. She feels alive with possibilities in a way she hasn't felt in years.

"I love you, Missy," Zach says.

Missy looks down, wiping away a tear.

"I can't believe I am getting so emotional," she says. "I guess it's just that not much good has happened to me, for a long time. It all feels too good to be true."

Zach pulls her in close and brushes her hair back from her face. "When I say I love you, I mean it. You are my home. I want to build a life with you."

"I love you, too," Missy says.

Zach can feel her chest rising in rhythm with his and smell the floral scent of her perfume as he leans in to kiss her softly on the neck. She pulls his body closer to hers as he kisses her deeply. They lie together on the beach blanket, Missy's leg draped over his, her head on his chest, and watch the blue sky turn to pink and then orange, until the sun drops behind the mountains and the stars begin to dot the sky.

Chapter 22

Zach pulls into the Inn the next day and takes the last space in the parking lot.

Stepping inside the Inn, he can hear the chatter of the guests lingering over breakfast and making plans for their day. Weaving between staff members who are rushing about, he asks where Missy is. Without even stopping, a young woman points to the great room.

He finds Missy on top of a ladder, hanging baskets of bright pink and purple petunias along the edge of the covered deck. He holds the ladder steady for her until she climbs down, then greets her with a big hug.

After hanging the decorations, they arrange a relay race and water balloon toss on the back lawn and set chairs around the fire pit for s'mores. Standing back, they're happy with their work, ready to enjoy the Sunday welcome picnic the Inn hosts for it's guests.

"It looks perfect!" Missy says with a grin.

"I don't know how you do it," Zach says taking in all she has done to make her guests stay at the Inn special.

The smell of the grill heating up wafts through the air as the staff brings out platters of watermelon and pitchers of iced tea and lemonade.

"Let me help you with those," Zach offers, taking the platters of watermelon over to the food tables near the grill, where his dad is starting to make hamburgers and hot dogs.

"Missy told me about you and Catherine," Zach says. "I'm sorry."

"Me, too," Blake mutters, not looking up from the grill.

They work in silence to prepare the food as guests start to fill the back lawn. Parents are setting up their beach blankets down by the lake's edge. Kids are trying to wriggle away from their parents, lathering them in sunscreen before playing lawn games.

Missy sees Catherine arrive and waves her over to where she is running a water balloon toss with the kids.

"Everything looks amazing," Catherine says to Missy.

"Granddaddy would be proud," Missy says, as they watch Emma tossing water balloons.

"Is this too awkward?" Missy asks.

Catherine looks over at Blake flipping burgers on the grill and shakes her head. Just weeks earlier, she had hoped their relationship would be forever and had even fantasized about marrying him, but it wasn't meant to be. While she is sad for things to be over, she isn't mad at Blake.

"No, it's ok," Catherine finally offers.

As the last balloon pops and the game wraps up, the kids run over for snacks at the food tables while the adults wander over to the volleyball court, where the adult game is starting.

Missy and Catherine decide to cheer on Blake and Zach, who are playing in the game.

Zach spikes the ball, scoring the winning point for his team. He runs off the court and scoops up Missy and spins her around.

"Don't drop me," Missy giggles as he sets her down with a kiss. "Oh, my goodness, there they are," Missy gasps.

"Who?" Catherine asks.

"The Jackson family. Zach invited Joseph and Karen and their kids to join us today," Missy explains.

Missy smiles and crosses the lawn, introducing herself to Karen and showing his kids the way to the games.

She brings Joseph and Karen over to meet Catherine, and they all join Zach at a picnic table in the shade, where they have a view of the kids.

"I hope you're enjoying your stay," Missy says.

"It's lovely," Karen says. "I've been telling Joseph for years that I wanted to visit Pine Lake. How long have you lived out here?" she asks.

Missy tells the Jacksons how she grew up spending her summers at the Inn with her grandparents, and that she moved here full-time before having Emma.

"It seems like you and your grandmother are very close," Joseph says.

"Yes, especially since Granddaddy passed last winter," Missy says.

Joseph nods, and shares that he was also raised by his grandmother. "Family is so important to me," he says, smiling. "In fact, one of the things that impressed me most yesterday is how Ya-Ya's pies are all about bringing family and communities together. I think our customers will really like this, too," he says.

Missy looks at Joseph. "Are you saying you want to work together?" she asks hesitantly.

"Yes. I want your pies on store shelves up and down the East Coast in the next thirty days. Then we'll talk about our plan to head west."

"Oh, my goodness! I can't believe it. Thank you so much," Missy says, shaking his hand across the table.

"My office will draw up the papers and send them over to you next week," Joseph says, grinning. "Now, enough about business. I think Zach mentioned something about a cornhole tournament?"

Zach and Joseph join Blake at the cornhole boards while the ladies head down to the beach for some sun and gossip.

Missy relaxes on her sun lounger and closes her eyes, listening to the murmur of the guests in the background as Catherine and Karen get acquainted.

She lets her mind wander, imagining Zach's hand in hers as they walk by the lake. He's in a pair of chinos rolled up at the cuffs and a loose-fitting T-shirt. She's in denim cutoffs and a white tank top. Emma is walking a little way ahead, collecting rocks; she loves the little pebbles on the edge of the shore that have been smoothed from the water washing over them.

Missy's resting her head on Zach's shoulder before he suddenly picks her up and starts running toward Emma. They are all laughing as he dangles Missy over the water, threatening to drop her in as Emma splashes her.

Setting her down in the shallow water, Zach brushes a curl behind her ear and kisses her softly. Wrapping his arm around her, the three of them head back.

She sees the Inn ahead of them, nearly twice the size of what it is now. All the rooms have balconies overlooking the lake. The back deck is expanded into multiple levels, stretching out across the expansive lawn. She sees guests docking their boats, playing on the private beach, relaxing on the deck.

She feels a tear roll down her cheek and opens her eyes.

A gentle breeze blows, and she can smell the lavender from the garden.

She looks back at the Inn, and she feels it. It's happening. Everything she has dreamed of and once thought out of reach is unfolding before her, and it's happening with Zach.

What began with her grandparents and a single lavender plant is becoming a beautiful garden.

Acknowledgments

My heart is full of gratitude as I sit down to thank so many of you who have supported me on this journey! Alexa, you kept me well stocked with beautiful notebooks and pens, without which I never could have written this story. You have taken me on hikes to clear my head, given me story ideas when I was stuck, and most of all, you have believed in my dreams and encouraged me to keep going when I was tired. Emily Tamayo Maher you have taught me to follow the synchronicities and you have supported me every step of this journey. Without you, this book would have remained locked away in my heart and my journals. To the team at Woodhall Press, I am so grateful for your expertise and professionalism. Ella, Jessica, and Amy, thank you for being such an amazing team and cheering me on and celebrating with me. My friends and family for checking in on me during the writing process. And, my fur babies, especially Iris and Dakota, who kept me company along the way.

About the Author

Katie Mongelli grew up in the suburbs of Washington, DC, but has always preferred the quiet of nature. Her debut novel *Finding His Way Home* captures what means most to her in life: family, love, community, and of course, cute lakeside towns. You can find Katie online at her website www.katiemongelli.com or on Instagram @katie.mongelli.